THE CLASS MERMAID

Published by - Spines
ISBN: 979-8-89569-924-9

THE CLASS MERMAID

Veronica Maria Tapia

CHAPTER 1

There was a voice, a call that nobody could hear or understand. This voice came from an unknown land, an unknown world below the seagulls' flight. But there is one teenager named Connie, an 8th grader who could hear the cries, who was confused at the beginning. The cries of the innocent had become part of her life. She wondered how on earth her father and brother would or could understand. The voices who cry will never go away until Connie saves them. Little does Connie know that the destiny that lies before her is shortly to arrive? And this is how the story begins...

The bell rang at Taylor S. Jr. High School in 1st period, ending English class. As soon as the class was about to get up from their seats, Mr. Gwodz yelled in a riot loud manner, lifting his head high, "The bell is for me—not for you!". He always says that line with an unusual accent. Connie is very worried about him. Sometimes, he spells words wrong, says words wrong, or even pronounces words wrong. Mr. Gwodz looked at everyone at their seat and declared, "Classsssisss dismissed." And he also has this strange way of extending his enunciation. Connie's classmates often wondered, "Where did they dig this guy up?" Everyone ran out as if it was raining inside the classroom.

It was time for 2nd period—math class. Connie usually meets her best friend Lydia outside in the halls. Connie had very light brown hair and green eyes.

"Oh, did you do your homework for math?" Lydia desperately asked Connie, "Because if I can't borrow it, why I'll just.... I'll just..." Lydia couldn't figure out the words, so Connie answered it for her because she has heard that line about a million times already.

"Die!" Connie answered with a groan.

"Yeah!" Lydia said surprisingly, "But how did you know?"

"Never mind," Connie said, giving Lydia a copy of her math homework out of her book bag, "We're gonna be late for class again."

"Oh, just a minute. Let's go to the bathroom."

"No. I have to get to class. And you're going to be late too."

"Come on! It'll only take a minute. You know how my lipstick gets faded."

"Don't I! Why can't you go by yourself?"

"Please," Lydia begged. "You know I don't want to go by myself."

Connie sighed. As they went into the bathroom, Connie heard the flow of water.

"Look." Connie told Lydia curiously, "that faucet is on." Connie went to the faucet, looking at it with a puzzled face. Then, she began to hear disturbing sounds. A voice called her name. She looked at Lydia, who was accidentally smearing the lipstick around her lips. Lydia looked in the mirror at her short brown hair and deep brown eyes.

"Yeah, Connie, do you still make those mermaid ceramics because if you do, I would like one or maybe ---"

"Shish. Listen.", Connie whispered to Lydia.

"What?" Lydia asked.

"Don't you hear something strange?"

"Yeah."

"You do?" Connie asked surprisingly.

"The bell hasn't rung yet," Lydia said thoughtfully. "Well? You haven't answered my question. Are you still making them?"

"No! I mean, don't you hear my name being called out?" Connie asked, desperately wanting her to hear... that voice.

"Yeah," Lydia said, "the faucet is calling you to turn it off. It is saying, 'Connie! Connie' turn me off! Connie..."

"Will you stop fooling around Lydia? Now, I'm telling you I heard something strange, and---

"Come on, Connie, turn off the faucet. You're wasting water." Lydia said, laughing.

"But I know I heard those sounds," Connie protested.

Lydia didn't pay any attention to her as she started to apply her lipstick.

The voice continued to get louder, ringing Connie's ears. She finally turned off the faucet.

"That's funny," Connie said confusedly.

"What's funny?"

"The voice went away."

"What voice?" Lydia asked, giving Connie a weird look.

"You mean... You mean, you still couldn't hear it?"

Lydia shook her head.

"You're still with that?"

"Anybody who's anybody could hear that sound a mile away! You must be deaf!" Connie exclaimed. She thought she was losing her mind.

"No," Lydia said, pointing her finger at Connie. "And you must be crazy."

"But I could have sworn that...."

"Come on, Connie. We don't want to be late for class. I don't know why you convinced me to come here."

Connie tried to convince herself that it was only her imagination. Besides, she thought, "If I heard it, why didn't Lydia?" She finally put it out of her mind.

"And you still haven't answered my question," Lydia said, "Can I have one of your mermaid ceramics?"

CHAPTER 2

Lydia and Connie were almost late to class. Connie sat down in her seat and tried to listen and pay attention to her math teacher. Actually, there was really nothing to listen to or pay attention to. Miss Woods was never a good teacher. All she ever did was pick up homework, give them homework, and not explain a thing, and as soon as she was done with that, she would go to her desk and eat her glazed doughnuts and drink her coffee. For once, Connie would like to have the principal walk in the class unexpectedly to see how awful Miss Woods looks and teaches. And every time the class has a test, Miss Woods walks around the class suspiciously, saying, "I'm watching you. No cheating!" with her eyes wide open. And when she hears a whisper, she turns that way from where she hears the noise and yells, "I'm watching." I'm watching you." Sometimes, she'll even use binoculars from her desk when her athlete's foot flares up.

When the bell rang, Connie frowned as she looked at her homework assignment because she did not know how she would do it in the world.

"Oh well," Connie sighed, "I'll ask my dad."

Everyone was already out of the classroom. Connie is usually the last one to leave the classroom.

"Goodbye, Connie." Miss Woods mumbles as doughnut crumbs tumble from her mouth.

"Goodbye, Miss Woods." Answers Connie as she walks out of the room.

Connie found Lydia in the halls with a bunch of girls. Connie had to tell Lydia how she felt about lending Lydia her math homework. She was so tired of doing her work for someone else.

"Lydia, umm...can I talk to you in private?" Connie asked.

"Don't be silly, Connie. Whatever you've got to tell me, it shouldn't be private to all my friends." Lydia said confidently.

Without any hesitation, Connie blurted out, "I don't want to give you a copy of my math homework anymore."

Lydia's eyes opened wide with anger and embarrassment.

"I know it's not your fault that I always give my homework, but I want to end this right now." Connie then let out a big sigh of relief as she got it over with. The girls giggled.

"Lydia," Connie said, giving her a weird look.

It looked like smoke was coming out of Lydia's ears. She let out a big scream as she hit Connie's foot with hers. As soon as Connie fell, Lydia and the giggling girls ran off.

Connie was hurting everywhere. "Why...why do I let her push me around?" She asked herself. As she got to her feet, she looked down on her bruised knee. It was red and bleeding through the cut.

"Oh, no," She cried as she put her hand over her head. "What's dad going to say?"

The bell rang. Connie knew she was tardy. But it was alright. Her next class was history, and her history teacher was usually pretty lenient. Connie quickly got a handkerchief from her book bag and put it on her cut. After the bleeding stopped, she ran to her class. Connie sat in her seat.

"I'm so glad you picked this time to join us, Connie." Miss Daniels said in a teasing way. The class let out a small laugh. Miss Daniels smiled at Connie, and she smiled back. Miss Daniels always seemed to cheer her up. Miss Daniels is so beautiful. Every boy in the class had a crush on her. Her green eyes always glittered. Plus, she's a great history teacher.

After history was art class. Connie is always looking forward to art class. There, she could express her ideas on paper. She loved to create her own image on anything. But she especially loves to draw anything that has to do with the ocean inside or out. Tables filled a classroom, and drawings, paintings, and picture finger prints covered the walls like wall paper.

"Mmmm", Connie sighed as she put her hands on the counter that was against the wall. She was gazing at her lovely painting of the sea. "I just love the sea," she said to herself. "I bet it is so peaceful inside." She said softly. "I wonder what it is like inside?" She rested her head on her hand and went to the other side of the room where her mermaid painting was displayed. The mermaid had long brown hair with a red tail that curled at the bottom of the paper. She had red lips, with her arms spread out. Connie could actually hear the waves of the ocean that turned to foam. She could feel the breeze blowing her hair back and breathe in the salty air through her nostrils.

"Connie!"

Connie gasped. "Oh—you scared me, Mrs. Mitchell!" Connie said to her art teacher.

"Why don't you take your seat," Mrs. Mitchell said, nodding her head.

"Yes, Ma'am, I will," Connie replied obediently.

"See that you do," Answered Mrs. Mitchell with her mean eyes. Connie has never met another person like Mrs. Mitchell. She had dark brown eyes with short black hair.

"It is time to illustrate anything that has to do with nature, and I hope you do a very good job since this is a very easy assignment. And Connie", Mrs. Mitchell added, "No more mermaids, huh?"

"Yes, ma'am," Connie replied.

Everyone was busy painting, drawing, and laughing. But most of the guys kept fooling around. One time, they put paint on

Connie's hair, and Mrs. Mitchell took her to the principal's office for fooling around in art class. Mrs. Mitchell thought it was Connie's fault. She sure protested that it wasn't, but do you think she can persuade a teacher who doesn't like her and that it wasn't her fault? No, indeed!

Connie was drawing her picture of the sea, minding her own business, while Mrs. Mitchell walked around the classroom looking at everyone's work. She finally caught Connie's picture in the corner of her eye with astonishment. She had never seen a picture of the sea done so beautifully done by a 14-year-old-girl. The seagulls soared in the air. It almost looked alive. Then the teacher caught herself with her mouth so wide open that a passing fly was almost her lunch. Mrs. Mitchell frantically gasped and gulped, attempting not to swallow the pesky UFO. Then she raised her chin high and walked off with a prance that said, "that didn't just happen to me." Connie giggled and giggled.

"Psss. Psss. Psss.," a young teenager named Bill, who sat across from Connie, whispered , trying to get her attention. "Psss!" Bill said loudly. Connie finally heard him and turned her head. She gave him a face that said, "What do you want?"

"I want you to sign something," Bill whispered with a grin.

"Why," Connie whispered back. She made it look like a bother.

"Please, just do it," Bill begged. He gave her the most pitiful doggy face that Connie had ever seen. Connie frowned.

"Okay,' Connie said, giving up. But she knew something strange was going on; she had never seen Bill act so nicely towards her since that time he put paint on her hair. He gave her a white piece of paper folded in half. She opened it. It was an ugly picture of Mrs. Mitchell! The picture had big eyes with a round body that covered the entire paper. It looked disgusting. And at the bottom of the paper were all the class names. Connie looked puzzlingly at the picture. Then she looked at Bill's smiling lips. Connie shook her head no. Bill nodded his head yes. "You're the only person who hasn't signed it yet," Bill whispered. But Connie kept shaking her head, no.

"Don't be such a wimp!' Bill said, trying to tempt her.

"No," Connie whispered.

"Yes."

"No."

"Yes."

"No."

"Yes."

"No!" Connie blurted out. Mrs. Mitchell looked up from her desk. The bell rang in Connie's ears. The class ran out of the classroom. They knew they would get in trouble.

Connie was just about to get up from her seat when Mrs. Mitchell said, "Stop!"

"I'm sorry I blurted out, Mrs. Mitchell." Connie held tight to the picture. Her heart was beating fast. *What if she catches me with this picture? Will she think I drew it?* Connie thought, *"Oh God. How do I get myself into these things? Please tell me what to do."*

Mrs. Mitchell rose from her seat and walked up towards Connie. "I'm sorry I blurted out, Mrs. Mitchell," Connie repeated slowly and then took a big, hard swallow. "Is that your assignment in your hand?" Mrs. Mitchell asked, her angered eyes following Connie's hand with the note. Connie was trying to hide it. But when she saw that she was obviously trying to hide it, she slowly put it back on her desk.

"No, ma'am, it's a ...." But Mrs. Mitchell wouldn't let her finish. Mrs. Mitchell picked up the picture. She opened it, saw it, and looked at Connie with the meanest eyes. Connie swallowed hard again.

"So," Mrs. Mitchell paused, "you drew this picture to let everyone sign it, but you didn't sign it, so everyone but you can get in trouble. Is that right, Connie?"

"Was that all one sentence?" Connie asked frightfully.

"Is it true?"! Mrs. Mitchell yelled as she banged Connie's desk.

Connie gasped because they were now almost touching noses. She bit her lips hard with tears running down from her eyes. Never had she seen her teacher so angry before. Connie thought her eye balls would pop out. Actually, the word angry is putting it mildly. Then, out of nowhere, Mrs. Mitchell smiled, walked away, and sat down at her desk.

"You may go." Mrs. Mitchell said. Her voice sounded shaky like she had a lump in her throat. Connie figured that it was the yelling that did it. She let out a big breath of relief. "But leave the picture there on your desk." Mrs. Mitchell added. Connie was too eager and too frightened to say good-bye when she left the room. As she shut the door behind her, she leaned against it, felt her head, and sighed again.

"Thank you, Lord." She said with relief. "Never again will I ever, ever talk to Bill. He's third grade mean."

Connie suddenly remembered it was time for lunch, something she usually dreaded. Almost every day, there was a food fight. She decided to skip lunch and hide in the bathroom. "Two more classes to go," Connie sighed, "just two more classes." She squatted down to decide how she could avoid Lydia.

After a minute or so, her knee started to hurt again. She hopped on one foot to the sink and turned the water on to clean her cut. Suddenly, she heard a distant voice calling her again. Connie could have gone to the school nurse, but she really did not want Lydia to get in trouble. Although-Lydia would not have done the same for Connie. The voice grew loud and louder still, as if in anguish.

CHAPTER 3

———

"Connie." The beautiful voice echoed, "We need you. We need you... we need you... Can you hear me? We need you..." Connie's breath sped up rapidly. She looked all around to see if anyone was there. As she heard the echoes, she also heard violence and voices screaming for help. Evil and danger surrounded her. Connie shook with fear. Terrified, she ran out of the bathroom, leaving the water running.

"This can't be happening to me," Connie said, shaking her head. The voice echoed one last time. The bell rang. Connie screamed, thinking it was the voice. But when she saw everybody running in the halls, she sighed with relief. It was time for science. She tried to get a hold of herself. It was only her imagination. She has been really stressed after all that's happened today. Stress, that's it. Still, Connie couldn't convince herself, "*It was so real... so real... that voice. And this wasn't the first time it called my name.*"

Science class was the same, as usual. Mrs. Harrison was always getting after the class for their misbehavior, especially Bill, the meanie. Yes, Bill is something else. But what Connie doesn't get is that the principal never expels, not even suspends that boy. Rumor has it that Bill is somehow related to the principal. "*Well,*

I guess it always seems good to know people in high places. I'll never know." Connie said to herself thoughtfully.

Connie was in class dazed at the very fact that she may be going insane.

"You hoo," Bill said with a high pitch, trying to get Connie's attention. She dropped down to earth and gave him a look.

"Leave me alone," Connie said angrily.

"Dang. Mrs. Mitchell must've really raised some hell, huh?" Bill laughed.

Yet Connie responded, "You're 3rd grade mean."

Bill was surprised that someone had called him that, for no one had ever compared him to a 3rd grader before. But he shrugged it off, walking away.

She was thinking about that voice. "*Where did it come from?*"

"Okay, class. I'm going to talk about the planet's rotation and revolution around the sun." Said Mrs. Harrison as the class settled in. "Write these notes that are on the board. We'll talk about them, and if you listen and participate, you should do well on the quiz tomorrow." Everyone moaned, but not Connie. She was still dazed at what happened in the bathroom. "*Is someone or something trying to get a message to me, but from where? Maybe some place we don't even know exists...*" Connie thought.

"Connie," Mrs. Harrison said softly, "Stop daydreaming and write those notes, please. You'll need them for the quiz tomorrow." Connie snapped to reality, took her notebook, and meticulously wrote her notes. Mrs. Harrison decided not to be too hard on her. Besides, Connie was one of her brightest students, and bright students are rare. And, anyhow, it doesn't hurt to be out in space now and then.

One of the things that Connie liked about Mrs. Harrison was that she was very understanding, reasonable, and practical. But, of course, she could never be any of those things to Bill. The bell rang. Drama! The last class, finally!

In drama class, Connie was still rousing in her imagination on where that voice came from. It was on her like glue.

"Class, I want you to read silently in your book of poems." Miss Thames said. She can be nice at times. Often, she smells like cigarettes, her hair, and her clothes. She's a little over-weight but attractive, though she often has circles under her eyes. One time the 8th period drama class went to the theater to watch Miss Thames in a play. The setting was in the 1930s. It was called "Enter Laughing". Connie enjoyed it. She was so surprised to see her own teacher wearing a long, silky gown that was low cut at the chest. Miss Thames is a very good actress---and a very good yeller in class. When she sees a student not doing what they're supposed to do, she will put down the entire class. She sometimes confuses the whole class, too. Sometimes, she'll give the class so many directions that not even she can keep up with them.

After theatre class is over, Connie (like everyone else) goes to her locker to get what she needs for her homework assignments. She usually waits for her father to pick her up at the parking lot. Connie was pacing back and forth. *"I know it couldn't have been my imagination. I just know it."* She still wondered what that voice was. It killed her with curiosity. *"I felt danger and evil. Danger and evil."*

Finally, her father, Mr. Thomas, came. Connie's father was short and always had a smile on his face. He drove a red 1988 Ford Mustang and often worked late hours.

"Another day of school! So, how was your day?" Mr. Thomas asked with a smile.

"Oh, I guess it was okay." Connie sighed as she got in the car. Connie noticed her father's eyes on her history teacher, Miss Daniels, leaving the building.

"I do believe that is Miss Daniels." He said with his eyes wide open. Connie had never seen her father get so excited whenever he saw Miss Daniels. "I believe you told me once, Connie, that Miss Daniels is single?" He asked.

"Yes, she is," Connie answered with a frown. *"I must have answered that question about a million times already,"* Connie thought. *"Well, I guess he likes to hear it, or maybe he forgets."*

"Hello, Miss Daniels!" Connie's father shouted as he waved to her.

"Hello, Mr. Thomas." Miss Daniels yelled back. Her eyes twinkled. She got into her car and drove off. Mr. Thomas was still waving at her.

"Dad, she's gone," Connie told him as she shook him.

"Oh, yes..." He shook himself out of his trance. "Do you think she likes me?" Mr. Thomas asked as he drove away. Connie didn't answer him. She was gazing outside of the window, thinking about the strange voice in the bathroom. As each minute went by, the voice in the bathroom became more unreal to her.

"Yes. She likes me." Connie's father answered himself, nodding his head. Then he looked at his daughter puzzlingly and asked, putting his hand over Connie's head, "Are you feeling okay?"

"Yes." Connie snapped back to earth. "I have some bad news." He told her, "I'm afraid I have to work late again, and you have to stay with Joey."

"Oh, no!" Connie pouted. "Do you have any idea what it's like having a sixteen-year-old brother who hears loud music all day and who also eats pizza all day—even for breakfast? He also thinks he's the lead singer in Green Day?"

"I know it's hard, Connie." Her father said softly, "but it's not the end of the world. I'm sure it's not as bad as it seems."

"Not as bad as it seems!" Connie exclaimed. "What do you mean it's not as bad as it seems? So you know what it's like spending all day with that creep?" Connie then looked at her father's face. It looked like his tolerance was running thin.

"I'm sorry, Dad." She apologized, "That was inconsiderate of me, knowing the many long hours you work. It's just that I have so much pressure at school and at home. And today... today I've been hearing strange sounds and I...." Connie suddenly stopped and realized what she was telling her father. *"I can't tell my dad that I heard strange sounds in the bathroom,"* she thought, *"he'll think I've gone nuts!"*

"Connie…?" Her father said, "And you were saying?"

"Nothing," Connie said, shaking her head. She tried to put a smile on her face. They were already at the drive way of their house.

When her father stopped the car, he put his hand on her head and shook her hair, saying, "I'll talk to your brother."

"Okay.' She answered with a lump in her throat.

As they started toward the house, already, the music was blaring. And the door was opened to the piercing sounds, which nearly burst Connie's ear drum.

"I told you," Connie warned her father. "That loud music is always on when you drop me off here."

"Well, I am going to put a stop to this, once and for all." Mr. Thomas said, walking up the stairs to Joey's bedroom door, yelling, "Turn off that radio!"

"I expect you to behave yourself," Mr. Thomas told his son, shaking his finger, "I'm going to work late again, and I expect you to keep an eye on your little sister."

"Yes, Sir", said Joey, swallowing hard.

"And take off that fake goat-tee. You look ridiculous!" His father protested, leaving the room.

"Connie." He said, knocking on her door.

"Yes, Dad?" She called out.

"I already talked to your brother." He told her as he opened her door, "And I don't think he will hear any loud music or wear fake goat tees any time soon."

"Okay," Connie said, simply smiling.

"I have to leave now," her father said, looking at his watch. And if there's any trouble around here, my office number is on the refrigerator. Connie doesn't know why he always says that. The phone number has been on that refrigerator door for over three years. Her father kissed her good-bye and left. Then Connie opened her eyes when Joey suddenly opened the door.

"Stop it, Joey!!" Connie said.

"Oh, is my little sister having a fit?" Joey said sarcastically.

"Leave me alone." Connie struggled to close the door. "You are so, so, so 3rd grade mean!" Then Joey let go of the door and started laughing. Connie shut the door.

Connie had a simple bedroom with her own private bathroom since she was the only girl in the family. She went to the bathroom sink to clean the cut on her knee. "Ouch," she said, touching it. She got a small towel, wet it under the running cold water and put it on her cut. As she was cleaning her cut, she heard the voice again. Connie was sure that it was the same mysterious, beautiful voice from school earlier that day. *Oh, no. Not again.* "Connie... Connie...." The voice called. Other voices began echoing around her, louder and louder. Cries for help surrounded her. Connie put her hands over her ears. She screamed.

"Connie! What's wrong?" Joey asked at the doorway of the bathroom. "And why were you screaming?"

"I don't know," Connie replied deliriously. She held her hands to her ears and fainted. Joey caught her and struggled to place her on the bed. He then ran into the bathroom to get some water and tripped on the wet towel on the floor as his back hit the hard tile floor.

"This is what I get for helping my sister?" He asked himself as he tried to get up.

After an hour Connie opened her eyes and gazed at her brother sitting at the edge of the bed.

"What happened?"

"I was hoping you could tell me," Joey answered. "I mean, you just fainted, and thanks to you, my back is killing me! Remind me to tell you to add a carpet in your bathroom because I never knew getting water could be so dangerous."

Connie smiled and began to laugh.

"You mean you fell?" She laughed even harder. "You big dope!"!

"Okay, okay. But I'm never going to fall for you again." Joey jokingly warned his sister.

Then Connie became quiet.

"It was so strange."

Joey, uneasy from the silence, interrupted her thoughts. "Well, I don't know about you, but I'm going to call out for some pizza."

"Wait for me!"

The brother and sister raced each other down the stairs.

Half an hour later, Joey was sitting on the couch devouring pizza smothered with pepperoni and cheese. The sight of this alone made Connie want to puke. *How can he eat that stuff every single day?*

"So, what's new in school? Joey fumbled out the words, still chewing his pizza.

"Nothing, do you mind if we don't talk about Lydia either?" Connie asked uncomfortably.

"That's cool. He paused. "Then... do you mind if we talk about mom?" Joey asked, trying to make a joke.

"That wasn't funny."

"Well, I'm sorry". He threw the half-eaten piece of pizza on the coffee table. "I mean, here I am trying to cheer you up, and all I hear from you is a bunch of wishy-washy stuff."

"No. I'm sorry." Connie said softly. "It's just that today, Tuesday–well, today is just indescribable. What I'm trying to say is that today was a weird day, and talking about mom is hardly relaxing."

"Alright, we won't talk about Mom. But will you do me a favor?" Joey asked. "Don't act like somebody just died."

Connie smiled, saying, "You know, I guess you're not as bad as I thought."

"Yeah, thanks," Joey said sarcastically, sounding grateful. He put the pizza back into his mouth.

Chapter 4

—————

After studying and doing homework, Connie had a restless night when she tried to sleep. It was sprinkling outside. The voice kept calling her all night. She tried almost everything to stop it, earplugs, turning the music loud, covering her head with a pillow. Nothing worked. But this time—she didn't just hear the crying voice. She felt it inside of her. When she woke up the next morning, she found herself in an awkward position. She jumped out of bed and hurried into her clothes, brushed her hair and teeth, and rushed downstairs with her books under her arm. She found her father in the kitchen drinking coffee and reading the morning paper and her brother (as usual) eating cold pizza from last night.

"You look very sleepy. Didn't you get enough sleep?" Connie's father asked.

"No, Dad." She answered, yawning. "But do I really look that bad?"

"Yeah, you look like Medusa!" Joey said, bursting out laughing.

"Will you leave me alone?" Connie told her brother.

"No, seriously," Joey said. "I heard you pacing back and forth. And I think I heard an orchestra, too."

"You're right!" Connie replied. "That orchestra you heard was my radio."

Joey gave her an ugly look.

"Is that true?" Her father asked, sounding concerned.

"Yeah, but Dad," Connie assured him, "I'm alright. I guess it was just one of those nights. That's all."

"Hey, Connie," Joey told her, "Next time you put that wimpy music on, warn me ahead of time so I can wear some plugs earplugs."

"Oh, save it, pizza breath!"

"Ok, you two, that's enough. Now, if you don't want to be late for school, I suggest we go now." Their father said.

Days went by. Connie had grown accustomed to the endless cries. And each time she heard the cries, her ears had opened more to the flow of water. Although she was frightened by the unknown, she was all the more curious. Her curiosity began to overwhelm her until one Friday...

The raindrops poured hard against Connie's bedroom window. The cries became louder than ever when suddenly a loud thunder shook her window. Connie woke up, soaked from her sweat." *What is wrong with me?" she asked herself.* She covered her ears with her hands as tears rolled down her cheeks. "What do you want from me," she asked. And to her surprise, she finally got an answer.

"Connie," the voice cried. "Connie! We need you!" the voice echoed, "Come! Come to the body where the waves hit the rocks!" The voice almost faded away and then grew louder, coming back again, like the rise and fall of the tides. "Where the waves hit the rocks... below the flight of the numerous seagulls... Come!" And then the voice disappeared.

Connie's heart beats fast. She looked outside. The sun was rising. *"Already? Where did all the time go?"* She heard her father's steps in the kitchen downstairs.

"Good morning," Connie's dad said with a smile as she walked down the stairs.

"Umm...Dad. Do you have any idea where the waves hit the rocks?" She asked slowly and thoughtfully.

"What on earth are you talking about?" her dad asked as he concentrated on the morning paper.

"Well, what I meant to ask you is... umm, do you have any idea, do you?" Connie knew she made no sense, but she couldn't help it.

"Go ahead. Do I know what?" her father asked with a worried look in his eyes.

"What I meant to say is... do you know where the waves hit the rocks below the flight of the numerous seagulls?" Connie's dad looked into her eyes, wondering what on earth was wrong with his daughter. Then he answered, quite thoughtfully, "Yeah, well... that would be Sea Park on the beach, way at the end of town. There are more seagulls there than anywhere else."

"Great!" Connie said, surprised.

"Why do you ask?" her father wondered.

"Well, there's something I have to do there. Can you take me there tomorrow?" Connie asked.

"Sure." He told her. "I have all the time in the world. That would give me a good chance to go fishing."

Connie's mouth opened as her father went on. "Gosh... It's been a long time since I've been fishing. The salty air, the beautiful waves... although I might be a bit uncomfortable with all of those rocks,..."

"Dad, Dad, Dad!" Connie said, trying to stop him, "Dad, you can't go with me." She said, shaking her head.

"Why not?" her father asked. Connie paused, wondering what excuse she would have to bring up.

"Well, umm... you know about my science project?" She asked him quickly.

"No. I don't. Do tell me," Connie's dad asked as if he knew his daughter had something up her sleeve.

"Well... in my science class, we are talking about oceanography," Connie lied quickly, "And what we have to do is that, umm, we have to count how many waves hit the rocks in thirty minutes."

"I do understand what you have to do," her father said doubtfully, "But what I don't get is why can't I go?"

"Well, Dad," Connie hesitated, biting her lips, "your fishing pole will decrease or increase the number of waves I count, and that will be the wrong count of waves."

"That is the most ridiculous thing that I've ever heard." He said, giving her a look, "Don't you think that's..."

The kitchen phone rang, interrupting his train of thought.

"I'll get it," Connie's father said, still giving her a look. "Oh, hi, Jerry," he exclaimed. Then he paused to listen while Connie wondered what the conversation was about.

"Tomorrow?" He asked disappointingly, "Well," he sighed, "That's life." He paused again, then let out a big laugh. "Yeah, I'll remember that, Jerry. Yeah, Okay. I'll see you at work."

Jerry must have said something hilarious, for her father was still laughing when he hung up the phone.

"Well, Connie, I guess you have to go without me," he announced. Connie smiled with relief.

The next day, in the late afternoon, Connie heard a big crash in the parking lot. Connie ran outside to see what it was. To her surprise, she saw her brother, Joey, in her father's car with a giggling girl in the driver's seat.

"Are you crazy?" Connie screamed, "Dad is going to kill you!" Connie was absolutely frantic. Joey got out of the car.

"Relax, sis," he said, calmly patting Connie on the back, "I've got it under control." He looked back at the girl, giving her a smile.

"Thanks for letting me drive, Joey. And I'm sorry about that just now." The girl in the driver's seat said as she got out of the car.

"Oh, that? Umm...no problem. Wait, don't you want me to drive you to your house?"

The girl gave a small laugh.

"Don't worry, I'm just down the block."

"See you on Monday?"

"Yeah."

Connie couldn't believe her eyes. She'd never heard her brother sound so nervous. She saw his eyes follow the girl until she was out of sight.

"You like her, don't you," Connie teased.

"What are you talking about? She's just one of my priceless, beautiful women."

"Whatever," she replied, laughing to herself. "But just wait till Dad hears about this. He's going to hit the roof!" Connie marched into the house.

"Wait! Wait!" Joey shouted, "What about the beach?"

"What about it?" Connie asked.

"I thought you told Dad that you had to go to the beach for a science project."

"So?"

"Well, Dad lent me the car to take you," he explained.

"You mean he knows that you have the car?" Connie asked.

"Yes, of course! Do you think I stole it, your big dope?" Joey said.

"So Dad gave that girl permission to drive, too?" Connie retorted.

"Oh... her...well, she needed a ride. That's all." Joey looked again in the direction of the girl who had walked away.

"I can't believe this is happening! Connie exclaimed. "My big dork of a brother is in love!"

"Hey, cut it out!" Joey covered Connie's mouth with his hand, which she bit wholeheartedly.

"Ouch!" He exclaimed. "Come on, Connie. Don't tell Dad I let her drive the car. "Remember that time you fainted?" Joey asked, pleading with her.

"So? What does that have to do with anything?"

"Well... I helped you. And you said that I wasn't as bad as you thought. You said so yourself. Just don't tell Dad."

"Alright."

"Alright! Let's go."

CHAPTER 5

Connie was finally alone at the cliff of gushing waters. Her brother Joey said he'd pick her up in an hour. And yet Connie paid him no mind. The sunset, and the breeze blew as Connie was walking to the cliff that led to the rushing water. She looked all around her, feeling that something was about to happen. Something extraordinary, something that she would never forget, was about to occur. Connie took a deep breath, breathing in the ocean's breeze through her nostrils. From a distance, she could hear a seagull's cry coming right at her. A beautiful white seagull flew up behind her, knocking her down. Connie gasped. The seagull squawked as it flew around, circling her. Connie tried to cover her head and face. She squinted, almost crying. When she felt that she wasn't being circled, she looked up, and there was the seagull, looking right at her, face to face. The seagull cried and squawked as its eyes pierced Connie's. Its wings flew like an eagle over a cliff. Connie quickly got to her feet and ran to the edge of the cliff. She looked over the cliff; she saw the seagull's claw at a big rock in the shallow water.

Out of curiosity and to get a closer look, Connie took off her sandals to climb down the cliff that led to the sea. As Connie was climbing down, she could hear the seagull crying louder and louder, covering up the sound of the waves. Climbing, she went closer and closer. The seagull hushed. Connie slowly touched the tip of its head. Its soft, white feathers felt soothing to Connie's fingertips.

"I think I'll keep you as a pet," Connie said softly.

The seagull's head kept moving.

"Are you telling me no?" Connie asked, laughing. Then, it flew away to the sea. Connie waded more into the shallow water, saying, "Come back!" But the seagull still flew on until it was out of sight.

Connie sighed, for she felt that she would never see the seagull again.

"Connie, Connie." The voice whispered. Connie's heartbeat faster and faster still. She remembered the same voice that was frightening her. The voice echoed, making Connie believe more and more that it was very nearby. Taking a deep breath, Connie clumsily walked on, farther out, away from the shore. When the water was up to her waist, she saw from a distance an extraordinarily beautiful woman in the moonlight. The strange woman had dark purple eyes that looked blue to Connie. Her skin had a different color, not at all like that of a human. It was a dark, creamy peach color. And her facial features were perfect and smooth. She wore a necklace of pearls and glowing flowers. Her wet, long, shiny hair was jet black. She wore many pearls, which dangled down the side of her ears, and shells covered her breasts.

Connie gave her a strange look. She never expected to see a woman in the sea, especially at night. She felt afraid, uncomfortable, surprised.

The strange woman's red lips smiled at Connie. The woman seemed sweet and friendly. Connie slowly returned her a smile filled with confusion.

"Are you the one who kept calling me" Connie asked, as she slowly came closer.

"Yes, Connie, I am." She answered. "My name is Norma, and I have come to see you, Connie."

"You have?" Connie was perplexed. Her heart was beating faster and faster, for she didn't know what else to expect. "Why?"

"Please, come closer. You seem so far away." Norma requested. Connie gave her another strange look. "Please," Norma asked again.

Connie turned to see if her father or brother were there. When she didn't see them, she turned her head back slowly.

"I... I guess it will be alright."

Connie hesitated, giving Norma a shy smile. Connie came closer. But in her second step, her left foot landed on something sharp. She screamed with pain and splashed into the water. Nora dived in to help Connie. As Connie picked up her head from the water to breathe, she suddenly saw a huge fishtail with fin high in the air, splashing into the water. Connie screamed and backed away. The pain of the cut on her left foot kept bleeding. As she backed away, she stumbled, falling again into the water. The saltwater choked her as she still screamed. Connie felt like she was going to die. When she reached the shore, she was still screaming and backing away as she floated on her back. She went too far, hitting her head on the huge rock on the shore where she pets the seagull. She was knocked unconscious. Norma swam to her rescue. She used some seaweed to heal Connie's wounds on her foot and on her head. She placed the seaweed on her wound, and then she waved her hand over the wound and Connie's wound directly healed. And then she waved her hand over Connie's head, and she felt immediate relief. "Why Norma, how did you, how?"

"Well, Connie, we have come from the land of Marrina, below the seagulls' flight, can heal humans. For some reason, I don't understand, but we can't heal each other." Norma said softly. Then Connie slipped into a mild unconscious state again.

"Oh, Connie, there is so much, so much you can do for us", Norma sighed. "Hopefully, you will agree."

Drops fell from the ceiling to the water of the unknown cave where Norma placed Connie. Glitter was on the ceiling and on the sides of the cave. The glitter reflected on the water like a mirror. Norma had laid on the rock that was in the middle of the shiny cave. Connie's head lay on Norma's tail. Connie mumbled in her sleep, shifting her head back and forth. With the palm of her hand, Norma rubbed Connie's forehead, rubbing off the drops of water that landed on her head from the ceiling.

"Daddy, Daddy..." Connie mumbled deliriously. "I had such a nightmare. I dreamt I saw... I saw... a woman, a strange, beautiful woman. Oh, Daddy, I am so glad you are here."

Norma sadly picked up her head, thinking that it was horrible to give her such a scare. Connie's breathing was heavier than usual. As Connie's eyes opened, she saw a blue, glittering light.

"Daddy," Connie called, "Daddy, where are you?" Connie's eyes were wide open. "Where am I?" She sat up, then she saw Norma's concerned face and hopped right off her long, beautiful tail.

"It's you," Connie said, breathlessly backing away again. "It's you! Oh my God, it's you! You stay away from me, or I'll...I'll scream,. That's what I'll do!" she warned hysterically.

"Please, be careful, Connie, you just had some trouble standing," Norma said gently.

Connie banged on the walls of the cave, crying desperately for help. She cried and screamed until there was nothing left of her. Her eyes then fell upon Norma's fishtail. Then, she suddenly became silent.

"You're ... you're a... a mermaid?" Connie said in amazement. "It's unbelievable! No, it can't be. I know I'm just having an intense dream, and I haven't woken up yet. So I will just be calm." Connie settled down. Then she looked at Norma, "You're still here?"

"Connie, Connie, please believe that I never meant to scare or hurt you," Norma replied.

"This can't be happening," Connie said, shaking her head. "It can't. Oh, God! Please tell me this is a dream." Connie again burst into tears.

"Please, Connie, listen to me!" Norma cried, "I never meant

to hurt you!" Guilt was in Norma's heart. "We need you, Connie, so desperately!"

Connie then realized it wasn't a dream. This was all strangely real.

"Oh, Connie, the cries of the innocent have brought you to me-my cries."

"What?" Connie asked.

"Please, try to believe me," Norma begged.

"That was your voice? That was you? Connie asked, wiping her tears.

"Yes. It was."

"Why? Why did you have to scare me like that?"

"I never meant to scare you, Connie."

"And how did you know my name when I haven't told you yet?"

"My own kind knows everything about you, dear Connie. We have been waiting for you, waiting for you for so long." Norma said gently.

"What do you mean waiting for me," Connie asked defensively.

Norma then reached out her loving hand, which seemed so peaceful. Connie's eyes met Norma's. Norma's eyes were deep and full of mystery and wonder, but they were also filled with sadness and great anguish. Connie felt such magnetism coming from Norma and a dangerous curiosity. Not in haste did Connie finally reach out her hand, but finally, in trust, she united with Norma, heart to heart. And at the moment their hands met their hands together glowed with a brilliance that caused Connie to gasp at such a sight. Then Norma said sweetly, "I will show you a vision, for there is no way I can explain." Connie's eyebrows wrinkled in question and confusion.

"What in the world is she doing to me?" Connie asked, thinking to herself as she stared down at Norma's glowing hand. As if listening to Connie's thoughts, Norma replied, "Close your

eyes and think nothing." Connie hesitated, then forcibly shut her eyes, thinking to herself,

"I must trust her. I must trust her. Who else can I trust at this time?"

Then, breaking away her thoughts, Norma gently replied, "I will place my fingertip in the middle here." And, with ease, she placed the tips of her fingers at the center of Connie's forehead and erased the tension from her eyebrows.

At first, Connie saw nothing but a bright light ahead. It was a long, hollow and dark round cave or surroundings---she could not quite make it, but she knew in her heart through the vision that there was a light, a light more grand and brilliant than any light she had ever seen before. Even brighter than the pathetic light of the sorrowful sun. Then, the light suddenly opened to a brand new world! Connie let out a big gush of breath and a smile of delight. Then, her mood strangely transformed. There was something greatly amiss. This world was not peaceful. It was surrounded by the darkness of all the forces of death. It was in the sea where danger and evil seemed to be slyly lurking. Connie saw a village, a village full of despair and violence. The sea rumbled with the cries and screamed that were reaching out for the energies ripped of life as Mermen masked in black in tall sea horses tore down their homes and massacred everyone in sight.

Explain more! Why are they killing everyone in sight? Connie was so frightened that she opened her eyes, gasping, "It's horrible! It's horrible! How can anyone do that to such, such innocent people?" Connie asked, lifting herself up in disbelief.

"It is all the works of the witch," Norma said sadly.

"What witch," Connie asked, wanting so desperately to know.

"Black Eyes of Edom, she is the cause of all our sorrows."

"Can't she be stopped? She must be stopped!" Connie exclaimed.

"That is my purpose of seeing you, Connie so that Black Eyes of Edom can be stopped," Norma explained. "I am the servant who has come for your help."

"But what can I do?" Connie asked in bewilderment.

"Oh, Connie, you are a wonderful human! Sometimes, you don't know what one human being can do for others. You believed in me. You believed in mermaids. You are the only human out of your whole world who allowed imaginary thoughts to come to life, Connie. You alone could hear our cries for help. So, you alone can help us. You alone are our hope, the savior of our land, Marrina."

Connie shook her head.

"No."

"Yes, Connie. You." Norma gently cupped Connie's face with her glowing hands.

"This has happened so suddenly, and I can...can hardly believe it, but...how could you expect me to save this...Marrina...You do understand that I am—

"You are human, a mortal."

"So how could I even get to this place, or even survive unless..." Connie's eyes penetrated deeply into Norma's eyes. "Unless... I become..."

"Like me. A Marrian.

The mermaid saw through Connie's heart and knew she could no longer fill the void of the cave with words. What could such a young, human girl say, after all? So she ended the long silence with the words that Connie had already anticipated.

"You must become like me. That is the only way you can survive below the surface of the water. If you decide to save our world..."

Norma then took a deep breath to prepare for the question she poses for her people: What is the destiny of the merpeople of Marrina?

"Will you save my world?"

Connie felt a big lump in her throat. She could run, but there was no escape from Norma's words. She could say no, but she would feel guilt flow through her human body. *"Could this be my destiny?"* Connie asked herself, *"Is this my destiny to save lives from another world unknown to man? Is this my chance to prove that I am worthy and that my life has meaning? And what about my father and brother? My father would think I'm dead. I don't want to put my father through my loss, to relive again the sorrow and the pain of five years ago when we lost Mom. But can I deny Norma or deny ever seeing her? Can I deny her needs and that of the Marrians?"* Connie tried to reach deep into her heart to say yes, but her fear overflowed her entire body. She had the fear of risking everything, most of all, the fear of risking her own life. Connie simply could not bear it any longer.

"Yes. Yes, I will," Connie burst out, "I will risk anything to save your world." Norma hugged Connie tightly as if she never wanted to let her go. Then this strange feeling overcame Connie, the feeling that Norma was omniscient, knowing all things, already knowing that her answer was to be yes.

All that time, while Norma was talking, Connie had her head down, trying to understand. Then, slowly, Connie lifted up her head ,looked straight into the mermaid's eyes and whispered, "Then that is my destiny. - to show the entire world that the fear of unveiling of an unknown world can be beaten."

"Connie, the time has come for your transformation. You must now trust me, truly trust me. It will be painful, and it will be uncomfortable." Norma took a small jar in hand. "I will fill this vile with my tears, and you will drink of it. This will temporarily make you a mermaid, a Marrian, but if you were to drink more than what I will give you, then you will remain a mermaid forever, but don't fear that won't happen." Norma proceeded to cry unto the mini jar which was a lot harder than she made it look. Her tears flowed easily, and then she grimaced and gasped for breath, exhausted. Connie's nose was red and cold. Norma flashed rays of light that contained all the colors of the rainbow on her skin. Connie swooned to the ground, losing consciousness and moving slightly. Norma looked on so regretfully, even she didn't anticipate that it would be this traumatic. She wondered if she had asked too much of Connie, for she was just a girl. Norma's tears continued to race through Connie's body, still jolting her to her very core. Slowly, painfully slowly, the enchanted elixir of tears eased and eased off and off from violating the corridors of Connie's teenage body. Afraid to open her eyes, the sound of the ocean filled her ears as if someone had placed the seashell close to her ear. A thin layer of skin covered the middle of the tunnel of her ears. Then, a thick red layer of skin flowed from her waistline to her toes, fusing her legs together. Connie felt a great source of pain and cried out, leaving her eyes still shut. Thoughts and memories raced through her mind during this metamorphosis. Then she felt a tremendous pressure throbbing in her eyes, forcing them open. When the transformation was complete, Norma said, "Come, Connie, to the Land of Marrina, where my people eagerly wait for your arrival." Following Norma's lead, Connie dove into the dark ocean and started a journey she would never forget with Marrina.

CHAPTER 6

After a day's journey, Norma said, "We'll rest here. We will sleep for a couple of hours. Now, don't be afraid; we will be safe in these waters." Connie lay down in frozen fear. Norma fell asleep right away. But Connie could not shut her eyes. Norma fell into a deep sleep with her beautiful head lying next to Connie's head. Connie became aware that she was in the strange wilderness. Her heart was beating faster and faster at the strange surroundings of her. As she looked at Norma, she noticed how beautiful she really was and, at the same time wondered why Norma's people needed her. What did they expect from her? A big question mark shaped Connie's face as she looked at Norma and thought about how mysterious this whole world was. At first,Connie only thought of herself as being in the sea with Norma. Yet slowly, she realized, "Hey, I now have a flipper for a tail. How awesome is that!" She felt exuberance and a carefree frivolity for merpeople innately are jolly. She danced and danced in the water. She performed maneuvers rivaling that of any dolphin. She flew through the water, jetting and diving and prancing. She was actually happy, like a jolly chicken of the sea. She was experiencing what it was like to be a mermaid, and she liked it! But as she was looking into her thoughts, Connie's eyes suddenly widened as a flash of light passed her. Frightened, she stopped thinking and wondered what that flash of light was. The instant flash looked like the tail of a comet in the space of sky. Connie sobered up fast. Now, again, she was nervous and frightened. She wrapped her arms around herself and asked, "What *could that have been?*"

"Oh, Norma, why did you leave me? "Connie cried out.

"Who said you were alone?" A little glowing fairy maid asked. The little fairy maid had silky wings and a mermaid tail like Connie and Norma, but she was so small, as small as a butterfly. Connie filled up her body with breath with, her mouth wide open, ready to scream.

"You wouldn't want to do that," the fairy maid snapped concertedly. "You're about to scare away the poor creatures right out of their wits!"

Connie was a funny sight as she asked, "Who, who...who are... what are you?"

"My name is Culpa from the land of Marrina. And I don't like..." She stopped suddenly, noticing Norma. "Princess Gwendela sent me to help Norma and you," Her snappy face turned sympathetic.

"Marrina," Connie said brightly. "You come from Marrina?"

Meanwhile, dark----dark, below the ocean, was a dwelling place of creatures that were slimy, dangerous, rebellious, and evil. Such creatures were unknown to mermaids. But, Black Eyes of Edom had a mysterious magnetism and controlling power over them, for the creatures claimed the evil princess as their own and followed and obeyed every command and desire of her evil heart. This dark, dwelling place in the deep sea was Black Eyes of Edom's abode. The Mermen were her dark minions subject to her might and power and evil whims. And at the moment, her attentions were to wreak revenge upon Princess Gwendela and Marrina.

Quickly, the vicious princess opened her eyes to the sight of a human being disguised as a mermaid. She was certain it was new to ocean life and a threat to her designs, and she grew angry. Black

Eyes thought and thought while she patted her obedient eel's head and rubbed down its long, scaly tail. Then, suddenly, a vision became visible to her like a small storm that opened and revealed the whereabouts of Norma and Connie. It was as if Black Eyes of Edom was looking into a crystal ball showing her a threat with the name of Connie. The sweet appearance of Connie, Norma, and the magical sea fairy Culpa caught the attention of her evil heart. She stared upon them, with her eyes pounding with such an intense anger, bitterness and hate. Then, slowly, she connived and lying back on her throne, she spread her arms with such laughter. She laughs, for she concocts deeds and tortures that she'll inflict upon unsuspecting threesome. The laughter vibrates the water around her with her fingers, both hands positioned as if to tear their flesh and rip out with her long nails their still beating hearts from off their chest.

"Culpa?" Connie asked with great confusion. "How or Why? I have so many questions I hardly know where to begin."

"You have been in the sea for one day, and night is covering the clouds now," Culpa explained.

Connie bit her lip as her empty stomach growled with hunger, *"Oh, how selfish I am."* Connie thought, *"Here I am, worrying my father to tears like he did when mom didn't come home. And I----I am only concerned about how hungry I am."*

"It is only natural," Norma interrupted, breaking Connie's thoughts. Norma had awakened, "As natural as the sun's reflection appearing from the deep blue seas."

Connie dropped her head with sorrow, looking at the waves that were straight, but then, as she looked down the long trail, she could see at a distance that the seemingly straight trail went down crooked.

All of a sudden, out of nowhere, for no reason at all, the water started to vibrate. Connie curiously looked up, but she heard a strange sound. It was as if the sound caused the water to vibrate. Connie quickly turned to Norma for support. She told her that there was no need to be afraid. Finally, Connie knew what the sound was. It was the sound of a dolphin, but she saw no sight of one.

Quickly, her heart skipped a beat. Norma revealed the secret to her. The sound of the beautiful dolphin came from her. From Norma! The sound, the vibration that came from her inner feelings of hunger, for a mermaid, sounded exactly like a dolphin; making the sound, the call for food, just the way a dolphin or a whale calls for hunger. Looking about her, Connie finally vividly caught sight of Norma. Connie's eyes widened as a whirlpool of fish, clams, lobsters, and many more came from the distance where Connie imagined them to be because of her hunger. Leaning back, she felt that the variety of food swirled around her. Her meal had come. Connie, through her psychic concentration, materialized. She approached the meal with delight.

"You looked into the distance, you were hungry, and from that distance that, you focused so intensely, that you willed your food to you. Now, that's one power I didn't imagine that you have!"

"What is this – there is Marrina." Connie exalted.

"You have also bent time short, and we see my land days before we're supposed to," Norma explained gently. Connie looked up and, to her astonishment, sighted the shores of Marrina. And she quaintly said, "O.K., but I suggest we eat first. First things first, you know."

Norma then said, smiling, "Yes, Connie (as she ate), somehow you knew it. You knew it was the Marrina, my precious home, Marrina. But you ignored your gifts, being blind to them. You had the feeling that Marrina and food were nearby as you looked with a focus with your own power, but Marrina is not in the open field of our world. There is a secret tunnel, that no human has been through or has seen. You also have a gift, a beautiful gift, of a sight that seems so unusual and hidden to humans. But you, Connie saw with loving eyes Marrina, and it opened to you to your heart, and that is why you willed Marrina close. That is why Marrina is before us now. You're a traveler that bends time and space. Time and space are yours to command. And as for the food that you will eat, you will not digest like humans, as in a mermaid, every protein in the food would not be wasted. The proteins left over will go to your soul. That's what makes our souls purer than humans. So Connie, never ignore your feelings. Search for them, instead of ignoring them, because," Norma paused, looking out towards the distance, "Marrina, we are here, which means that Black Eyes of Edom is close and threatens us."

Connie did not understand the last line. Norma looked troubled, but Connie knew that Norma understood so many esoteric matters. Norma always spoke the truth and always acted from the truth that abided in her heart. What many other mysteries Connie would learn she did not know. Then, looking at the variety of the food that encircled them, the three proceeded to feast all three not only enjoying their very tasty food but also enjoying each other's company.

As they ate, Connie felt a great sensation, feeling every blood cell take in the nutrition of the sea that made her feel stronger as she took each bite. Her mermaid tail no longer sensed the touch of helplessness and frailty. She was able to move her tail with great energy and power, with the ability to move her tail the way a mermaid should. And her soul felt loving, stronger than the winds that make the sea quiver.

"I come from where flowers glow brightly in the beautiful land of Marrina," Culpa announced with great character. "Here we live, we plant seeds, and the flowers glow, especially the Wheatigi."

"Wheatigi?" Connie asked, startled.

Culpa's eyes wrinkled, offended, as she said, "Yes! Wheatigi."

Connie then smiled, looking at Nora, who had been smiling all along.

"Wheatigi is the name of our flowers." She introduced the story she was about, to begin with, eyes opened big with pride. Culpa told Connie that she and her family have been cultivating the flowers of Wheatigi for centuries. Wheatigi is the source of food that all mermaids need. Wheatigi encapsulate all the nutrition that the merpeople and sea fairies require to be content.

As Culpa spoke, they all felt a bond of closeness making Connie feel closer to Marrina than ever before. Culpa then explained to Connie how and where in the meadows that Wheatigi is grown. The stems of the flowers are short but very thick, containing sweet, clear nectar. In the middle of the thick stem of the flower is a tunnel where all the small souls of sea fairies incubate, waiting to be born.

"The sweet liquid of Wheatigi," Norma said, continuing the conversation, "is what we and the sea fairies need to feed on and survive, for if we do not partake, we won't survive, and we will be no more. Our bodies have some human parts, origins, and the needs of humans ----- our bodies, though, are 99% of Wheatigi water."

Connie smiled astonishingly as if she were a scientist finding major and miraculous discoveries. After she had gotten over some of those feelings, she finally said, "You mean to say that — that Wheatigi is like water, and...." Connie couldn't get over the feeling of confusion, "And you are half-human, so you need water?"

"Look, Connie, we in Marrina, when we want to communicate with the surface dwellers, we talk into the flower of the Wheatigi as if it were a microphone. We talk into the flower in the hopes that someone will hear us. We don't know if we'll be heard, nor do we know who will hear us, if anyone. But I now know that you heard us, Connie, of all the surface dwellers on this planet, you alone heard us. That is why you are so special to us, Connie! Yes," Norma continued, "On earth's dry land, you often hear the flow of water, well to those who listen very attentively to the sound that the water makes, you'll hear our messages to the surface dwellers. Two examples are the murmur of a brook or the sound of waves as they reach the shore. If there were to be no Wheatigi, you could not hear us. Wheatigi makes it possible for us to communicate with you."

Connie suddenly felt trapped in wonder about how she was supposed to help their world, and she became nervous. She tried to put some thoughts together, but gears slipped and shifted in her mind, and something was wrong with the life of the sea.

"How am I to save your world?" Connie blurted out. Her eyes widened, surprised at her own curiosity that was anguishing within her, then erased her surprised look and tried to be firm. Connie's eyes followed Culpa's as Culpa looked at Norma's. Then suddenly, as quick as thought, Black Eyes of Edom is before them. She looms large and heavy and menacing, and she loves a good entrance."

"How dare you think you can come against me," as Black Eyes of Edom brandished.

"Why can't you tell me? Why can't you............" Connie stopped, feeling her stomach tremble and bent down. Ugliness and dirtiness filled her mind. Norma quickly went to her, holding her as tight as she could, trying to drive the ugliness and the nasty pain away. Norma picked up Connie's head, and with the palm of her hand, she felt Connie's forehead. Connie was feverish and hot. Norma gasped, bending down to feel her stomach.

"What's happening?" Connie thought to herself. Norma quickly picked up Connie's head, and as she looked at her face, an expression of fear flooded her. Norma tried to smile, looking into Connie's confused and tired eyes as she began to close her own eyes, Culpa swam to safety, hiding behind Connie.

At that instant, Connie felt thunder underneath the ocean floor. It grabbed her heart as she looked down at a long, curled, scaly, thick tail. Black Eyes of Edom appeared in front of Connie, who hadn't seen her yet. Then, the evil princess took Connie to her dark cave. Covering the Black Eyes of Edom's tail were strands of pearls, gold and silver beads dropping down from her, and it was her inoffensive excrement like those of a rabbit. The tail looked like a colorful snake, but Connie's vision was too choppy — too vague to tell. As Connie's eyes lifted, the shiny jewelry that covered her waist all the way up to her neck blinded her. Connie covered her eyes with her hand, but the princess's devilish grin was still there.

"I find that is very common among humans — they wonder. Like you," she stopped dramatically, "Yes, like you. You all believe in mermaids ---- and I wonder why!" the evil Princess retorted angrily. Black Eyes of Edom continued to torture Connie's mind!

Shaking her head, Connie couldn't take it anymore, wailing "No!" continually.

Norma was quite aware out what was happening, for she could tap into Connie's mind.

"Connie!" Norma cried telepathically, "Connie!" She sees her eyes, but they are blank.

"You mustn't try to communicate with her!" Culpa shouted, stopping Norma, "You must remember what and who you are! Your soul is too pure to touch a mind filled with evil." Norma started to cry, not catching the pearls at all. Inside the water, a mermaid's tears turn into pearls. "For if you do....we all will die." The odd pearls are gem like, beautiful but spiritually toxic.

"But she needs me! I love her so much! I do not want evil to touch her soul!" Norma sobbed.

"Your people need you, Norma. Marrina will deeply grieve and flounder if you die. Ever since Princess Gwendela took you in, the Marrina has loved you," Culpa explained.

"But I---------"

"Shhhhh, Norma, hush now, have faith. Connie will come back to us soon. Truly, Connie has the strength to face and defeat such evil, for she is a privileged human."

Chapter 7

Brooding dark clouds covered the evil Princess's throne. The Princess shifted the clouds to reveal her garish and evil person, yet the evil one actually possessed a beautiful face. She was a picture of such royalty and evil power. Connie could hear her breath as water stroked past her gills. She had beautiful black, curly hair, but at the same time, her face looked ready to attack. She sophistically positioned her body on the throne with her shiny jewels dangling down her forehead and with her long finger-nails. She was petting her pet lizard eel, which was also decked with jewelry.

Connie's scared eyes searched around her surroundings. The walls were mostly covered with blackish-green sea plants that seemed to move. Below the floor, caged creatures lurked to and fro. And fish with huge, sharp teeth were at every corner of the dark room. Black Eyes of Edom seemed to support most of the little light that was there. Connie's mind writhed with madness at the horrific sight, making the beautiful dark princess roar with animal laughter.

"Leave me alone!" Connie's thoughts pleaded. But the evil princess's animal laughter went on, louder.

Connie wanted to say it one more time but couldn't. Her

mind was in the hands of someone else, not letting her gather her own thoughts.

With relief, the princess suddenly stopped, but stopping too suddenly gave Connie more mental pain, but the laughter was gone, which gave her some peace. Connie looked at her face with fright, making her look away once more. The Princess's face turned angry, with such hatred in her fiery eyes, which looked wider with her high eyebrows as if they were to pop out. Her long fingered hands clenched to the arms of her throne. Connie did not want to see Black Eyes on Edom's face; never the less did, and she was filled with wonder and deep curiosity. Connie uncovered her eyes and saw shiny, red lips, a pale, smooth face, with devilish red eyes. At that sight, Connie's muscles loosened, but her bones shivered.

True, she was beautiful, with her gorgeous face and beautiful long, thin, black, curly hair, but her devilish grin and her deep fiery eyes left everyone who saw her affright. Connie was sure that she was looking right at her, but in reality, Black Eyes of Edom was looking at Connie only as an object, not as a viable living soul.

"Let your thoughts wander." Black Eyes of Edom suggested as she breathed deeply. Connie gasped. Her voice was so deep for a female, too deep. It was as if her voice pounded her heart, for Black Eyes of Edom's was adept at mind games and brainwave jamming.

"You wish I were dead, but I am not! I will reign forever, destroying Marrina, until the final destruction is complete." Black Eyes of Edom warned Connie's mind. She tried to jabber Connie's mind, making her realize how far she would go to do this.

"Let go of my mind!" screamed Connie. Tremendous pressure was forcing Connie to scream in anguish.

"Silence!" she worded with her teeth clenched. Then, that familiar, easeful expression appeared on her face. Connie was more at ease now.

"You did that just to torture me," Connie replied with the

little strength she had. With that, Black Eyes of Edom smiled, laughing with contentment, and then turned her head and looked the other way. Connie could now look at her but became startled as Black Eyes of Edom instantly turned her head back to look at her. Connie knew why she did this; she was playing a game that tricked her by looking the other way so that Connie could easily look and then get startled.

"You do not even know what torture is," she said, nodding. "You're just a child." Her eyes suddenly brightened, "But you will." Leaning more to enhance her look of anger, she said, "You will be nothing but a speck of sea foam."

Confused, Connie said, "You're lying."

Angrily, the lizard eel growled as it snapped its teeth, with its tail wagging rhythmically.

"Am I?" she said gently, leaning back on her throne. Looking at her pet, she smoothed its scaly forehead with her fingernails, calming it. "He doesn't seem to like your approach, Connie." Her voice sounded deeper than ever as if Connie had offended her creature, for to her, the creatures of her kingdom were one – always one. With a thoughtful smile, she asked, "You did not expect me to be beautiful, did you? I've seen it in your face before."

"I don't know. I don't think I remember ever thinking that" Connie said, trying to get a hold of her. Connie never knew anyone could change her moods so quickly.

With no expression whatsoever, Black Eyes of Edom cunningly answered, "Oh, but I know you do," allowing her beauty to shine. Subtracting that, she quickly became angry again, "Marrina was not the only kingdom that kept their eyes on you while you were still with your father. I, too......." she stopped with a smile, "The Kingdom of Edom and I looked upon you every day of most of your life." Not knowing this, Connie felt strange, realizing that both Marrina and Black Eyes of Edom were looking at her and her normal life of before. "So, you think that you have equal claims on me just the same as Marrina!?"

Anger filled her mind; not realizing this, Connie felt like she had been cheated out of the truth. "So, that's why neither Norma nor Culpa told me anything," Connie thought. "Norma was afraid of all that was going to be, afraid of my reaction at this moment."

"That's right!" The evil princess snapped, "Both Norma and Princess Gwendela kept that from you." Deeply laughing, she continued, "Oh my, you're just learning that now?"

Connie slowly looked down with contempt and wished that she had never come to this undersea world and also wished that she was with her father.

With hate in her voice, the princess scolded, "You don't even know how to save their precious world."

"You're right," Connie thought.

"Risking your life on account of that," her thunderous voice insisted. Black Eyes of Edom delightfully laughs at her. She leaned forward to make sure of Connie's discomposure, and then she slowly leaned back comfortably.

"I don't understand, I just don't understand," Connie said, wanting to cry but couldn't. Both anger and sadness filled her soul.

"Oh, you haven't begun to know it all," Black Eyes of Edom assured her with a demeaning glance, "Yet, you will. You will now see..." the vicious princess said, projecting destruction. As she uttered, the room became nearly pitch black, with her face blending within the blackness, and again Connie thought, "Destruction."

The room roared with the most evil of blasts and with that, the glow of a black/blue box appeared, and with the twist of a fingernail from each hand, it went in circles, making Connie catatonic. Her mind went blank, but her eyes frantically searched for Black Eyes of Edom.

The box suddenly stopped right in front of her darting eyes. A red laser of black opened 1/3 rd of the box from the bottom. In the opening, she saw a face with the red lips, smooth pale skin, and red devilish eyes. It was as if Connie had seen her for the first time, for she had an expression that Connie had not seen her use yet. Connie noted that Black Eyes of Edom had the attitude of that of a storyteller but of someone who was trying to tell her side of the story.

The box opened ¾ of the way open, making her face more apparent. And Black Eyes of Edom began her story, "In the land of Marrina, two mermaids were born – one named Gwendela, one named Matropula. Both were born of royal descent to co-rule Marrina with great majesty and beauty. They were to help Marrina grow stronger with fellowship and love that would bond everyone together, and there would be great harmony.

As they grew up, a sense of leadership grew inside them, even as they played childish games, all along being lovingly cared for and nurtured by their father, the King of Marrina. Their mother, their sad mother, on the other hand, was deathly sick and began to die. For a legend of the land told that one day, the two mermaid sisters would be born under a star of destruction and evil. And that the separation would tear them apart, leaving them enemies and that nothing could prevent it. The Queen never wanted to see that day come to pass. So, at the bedside of her deathbed, where she lay on a large gold encrusted magnificent bed, stringed with sea jewelry of royalty, the Queen conveyed her hopes and dreams for them that they love and respect each other no matter what. But scarcely had she begun when, in sudden silence, she died and withdrew. With great confusion as to why their mother had to die so soon, the two began to mourn her deeply.

As the years passed, the two sisters, who were so close, began to distance themselves, as the legend had predicted, making the king sad and disturbed. Princess Matropula was the one who began to grow dark inside and felt that she didn't belong to Marrina, or to her father and sister. They both tried to reach out to Princess Matropula but to no avail. She closed her heart and only ran further into evil, making her do strange things that were the opposite of what her parents taught her in "Marrina'. But the evil in her wasn't complete yet.

As her father grew older, Princess Matropula began to notice that love was in the waters. An affection of love was budding between Princess Gwendela and a young merman; they met in secret, for the king did not approve of losing Gwendela because he already lost his wife and one of his daughters. The thought of losing his sweet daughter Gwendela actually hurt him deeply. Matropula did nothing but watch the drama that was going on, not caring at all. Until one day, an evil ingenious plot came to her mind, initiating for the first time a sinister deed. She wanted to destroy their love and, at the same time, gain favor with her father, so she waited for the convenient time to pounce on her scheme.

Sometime later, the king became terribly ill. He was already old and tired yet still very distinguished. On one of the days of Princess Gwendela's secret meetings with her beloved, the father was in great pain and desperately needed relief to ease the pain. So Gwendela had to miss their engagement and tended to her beloved father. Matropula, disguised herself as Gwendela (for at this time, the sisters looked remarkably alike) and broke the merman's heart, telling him that she never wanted to see him again because she was in love with another merman and that she would marry him soon. As she was doing this, she looked up to see the merman lose his composure. His face betrayed- his anguish, he was tearing and looked oh so crushed.

Gwendela did not know what was happening behind the scenes. The merman sadly soon departed Marrina's waters.

As Princess Matropula approached the palace, she was met hysterically by her sister Gwendela, who was frantically asking her where she had been. Not answering, Matropula felt the satisfaction of seeing her sister desolate and having made her lover flee from Marrina.

"What's wrong with you?" Gwendela screamed, "Over the past few years, you have not been acting like yourself." Pearls of tears were rolling down her cheeks, "It's like you've changed so much."

Filled with rage, Matropula denied not acting like herself, and with that, she yanked herself free of Gwendela's hand and started laughing and leaving at the same time.

"Do you not care?" cried Princess Gwendela, "Do you not care that father is dying and that he wants you to be next to him too?" She then swam inside the palace, leaving her sister Matropula feeling like she had just been literally stabbed in the heart. Her heart bled tears, for she could no longer cry pearls; Evil had taken over.

Filled with a great desire for forgiveness, she quickly swam into the palace, wanting to change. She approached the royal room of her father's but suddenly stopped for she grasped the words on her father's lips. "You're to be my sole heir, the one and only Queen of Marrina - Gwendela". The King of Marrina, upon his deathbed, gave the power to rule over Marrina to Gwendela.

Matropula swam anxiously into the room to stop his words as Gwendela lovingly held the king's hand, for death was so near.

She quickly knelt by the bed-shell where her father lay and pleaded to her father's eyes that this could not be and to give her another chance. With great anguish, she leaned over the shell for his lips were to reply, but he was stunned by the sting of death and upon realization, that he could not speak. He simply smiled, then died."

Now, there was silence in Connie's ears. "But how can that be? Oh my God," she thought, "My whole body is here," she felt her human body, "But, how can this be when I am a mermaid? And how can I still be breathing normally in the sea? She looked in the box and was filled with the greatest of confusions.

"The truth has made you human, taking you away from the body of a mermaid, for as a mermaid, you were held back from the truth. I am now giving it to you: truth. Is that not what you want, Connie?" Black Eyes of Edom asked.

"But how?" Connie demanded from the evil princess.

"Silence!" she roared, making Connie gasp. Then, in sudden, unexpected gentleness, "Listen."

With that, the box closed, making a new opening, but this time it opened in the middle of the box, from which she continued the story...

"Then darkness filled the land at the death of the beloved King of Marrina. Lifting her eyes from her father, Matropula looked at Princess Gwendela with hate and jealousy. She blamed Gwendela for everything that had happened. She blamed her for the death of her father. She blamed her as well for stealing from her the rule of being Queen by manipulating her father with her lies, and then she proceeded to blame her for her mother's death. Crying, Princess Gwendela begged her to stop and said that it was not true.

Rising up with such evil indignation and bruised ambition, Matropula confessed, "I was the one that was responsible for the love of your life leaving!" Gwendela looked up in shock. "Yes, I did, and I will see to it that you're always alone and soon...with no Marrina."

Gwendela screamed in horror with full knowledge of what had just happened in her life, which made Matropula glad with satisfaction.

Then, with quick rage and ambition, blurted, 'I will create my own kingdom. There I will be the power, my own power, so powerful that Marrina will soon be mine! I promise that I will soon rule Marrina; but until then, while it is still your precious kingdom, I will make Marina feeble, and I will see to it that it becomes fragile. Then soon, you shall beg to surrender to me, me alone; and you, my dear sister, will finally be destroyed!'

Leaving Marrina to fulfill her promise, Princess Matropula wandered into the sea, traveling farther away from the land where she was born into royalty and finding a cave filled with dangerous creatures hidden from the land of Marrina. This was her new kingdom. Strangely, though, the creatures invited her adoringly, as if they had been waiting for her for a very long time. Evil completely filled her body, even in her breathing strokes of her gills. Evil shaped her pure tail into a long, thick, scaly snake tail, making her eyes black and dark with hate and red flames as her pupils.

She created her kingdom, she named it Edom, calling herself Black Eyes of Edom. With sinful pride, she announced her name to every living creature in Marrina during her acts of destruction where she raided and looted and only then was her name and new kingdom frightfully known in the land of Marrina."

Glenda was a witch, and it was her that taught Matropula the ways of sorcery and the dark arts. But being unwise, she taught herself. "There can only be one Queen of Darkness here. I will not chance that someday you'll do me in. So before you destroy me, I will destroy you. I will have no rival like I did before."

Chapter 8

Then the glowing box closed dramatically, leaving Connie in great awe as it landed back into the Black Eyes of Edom's fingernails. Then, the light within the box died.

With loving eyes, Connie lifted her head to the one who once was Princess Matropula, saying, "You are Princess Matropula, born in Marrina, sister of Princess Gwendela." She stopped and then pleadingly asked, "How can you be so cruel? How can anyone be so cruel?"

"It had to be done," Black Eyes of Edom snapped, then turned away as if she could not bear it anymore, biting her beautiful red lips. Wrinkling her eyes, she looked at Connie as if she really cared to reach out. "I just wanted to rule Marrina. Is there any harm in that? I was the oldest, and it was my birth right, and it was to be my legacy."

The vicious devil eyes, to which Connie was introduced, looked like a poor, lost soul to her. Noticing Connie, Black Eyes of Edom hardened her face, trying to wash away the obvious change in her expression, but Connie knew what the princess of all evil was doing. She was trying to paste a good soul that would show from her gorgeous face.

"You wanted to ask for forgiveness then? Why not now?" Connie asked, trying to reach out to her.

"It is too late. I'm too evil. I am drenched in an evil darkness that has already taken me over completely!" She snapped, angrily pounding the arm of her throne with her fist, which shook the room, "Ever since I left, Marrina," she said shamefully as she lifted up her head, remembering. "Do you think that there's anything left for me of a girl?"

She looked at Connie with the flaming pupils of her black eyes, which widened. It scared Connie and left her immobilized. She asked herself if this could really be happening to her. Could Black Eyes of Edom be trying to change and shift from her true self?

It suddenly dawned on Connie of this conclusion, but looking at the princess it gave her such sympathy at the thought of not believing in a poor, lost soul. She seemed to want to change from herself, but evil was holding her back. Connie came to believe and understand that Black Eyes of Edom wanted to become the little Princess Matropula that once was, before her mother died, and she wanted to be reunited with her sister Princess Gwendela.

"And both reign over Marrina until our end of time," the evil princess smiled, holding her shoulders with such longing, reading Connie's thoughts.

"Oh, would that not be such a wonderful, glorious, miraculous event to happen," Black Eyes of Edom squealed, looking like the happiest of children moved by the thought of a fresh, new beginning. Her eyes glowed with grinning, but Connie wasn't completely convinced.

Black Eyes of Edom considered turning Connie back into a human being for good, but Black Eyes of Edom considers a different ploy.

Black Eyes of Edom's cheekbones glistened with beauty, but she held it back very slowly as to look natural. She suddenly stops smiling and looks deep into Connie's eyes, shocked with sadness, as she covers her mouth with her hand and gasps.

"What is it?" Connie asked with concernment ,her eyes wide open.

"Your father," she replied, "your poor dear father, your father is in tears, worried over your disappearance and torn apart." She looks about the room as if she could actually feel beyond her kingdom, across the waters of the sea, into the earthly world. Sorrowfully, Connie's eyes followed hers, and to her surprise, Black Eyes of Edom created a reel reality like a video on the ceiling of the room, making her fall to her knees, almost gasping in turmoil. She agonized over her father, making her body fall limp as Norma called out to God for help, praying.

The magnificent hologram was made by the princess it was of the world and life that Connie inhabited. She had made an opening to the world that Connie was born in, and she offered her a chance to go back. "Now, Connie, how would you like to go back to your father to your life?" I can make it happen right now. Black Eyes of Edom snaps her fingers. Connie's neck was bent back, yearning, looking at her world above, on the ceiling screen, holding her arms outstretched as tears landed around her knees, calling, "Daddy, daddy, I love you, daddy!"

Smiling slyly, Black Eyes of Edom leaned back on her throne, filled with overwhelming confidence that Connie would fail Marrina. Alas, she shall rule Marrina, she alone, Connie, was to be a threat no more. The hope that Connie alone was to be the only possible savior of Marrina shall be based on the rocks of some distant shore. Black Eyes of Edom had completed her effort of acting out like she wanted to repent so that Connie would get confused – grabbing at Connie's human heart by telling her past life and of little Matropula, who was once kind,

"What a human fool Connie is" Black Eyes of Edom thought, "I understand the dark, black powers of hell! Oh my..." laughing within herself, "such ignorance."

The fire began to fall from the sky of Edom at the edge of its

boundaries, for in reality, Connie could return the world of reality, for only the touch of Connie's hand was needed to return her
to the sandy beach where it all began. It changed more than half
the atmosphere of the kingdom, which allowed fire to fall more
than halfway of the kingdom, but as it landed near the surface, the
balls of fire turned into steam mist with the smoke of tears from
Connie and the waters of the sea.

Then, unexpectedly, a wave of unselfishness gushed into her
body. It widened her eyes as she called for her father in anguish.
This caused her to gently bend over her knees as Black Eyes of
Edom was still thinking with evil. She had an overwhelming
fulfillment of the final destruction that would lead to total
control of the seas. "Nothing, not even God Himself," she
thought, "can stop me."

Meanwhile, the miracle of Norma's prayer came true as
Connie cried aloud, pouring out her heart and soul, "Daddy, if
you could hear me – I love you. I will see you someday, and I hope
you will understand. Do you hear me, Dad?" Her whole body
quivered, the cells in her veins vibrated vigorously; her nerves
made her heart beat faster and faster. The evil princess was
shocked as she thought that it couldn't be, that it couldn't
possibly be...Connie couldn't say farewell to the chance to finally
go back...she clenched her evil heart in suspense, and with the last
of her gasping breath, Connie whispered, "For I have to save
Marrina." With that, Connie fell face down, giving up on the
chance to go home. She sacrificed herself and the dearest desire of
her heart. The only opportunity she had in her hands, and yet
never foreseeing another, or so she thought.

The Kingdom of Edom was blacker than ever. The sounds
sent echoes throughout the cave, which was made by Black Eyes
of Edom herself were dire and frightening. Radically, she shook
the walls, severely causing chunks of rubble to fall. She turned her
into a wild beast, uncontrollably swearing that her day shall come
when Marrina shall become hers'. Connie slipped away and disappeared from the face of the evil one.

Tears intermingled with blood dissolved down Connie's eyes they came from her soul and her mind as she recuperated in Norma's arms. Connie's words to her father and her cries of pain from the first time she became a mermaid in the secret cave shifted, switched back and forth in her mind, as she anxiously awoke with her mermaid tail as weak as a wavering flower being blown by huge, strong gushes of wind.

"Norma?" Connie was finally able to say. When her eyes were wide open and awake, everything looked blurred as she looked at the pretty face of Norma, for she felt as though she was a newborn, which astonished her.

Hearing the rapid, frightened giggles stroked by Connie's gills and feeling her heart beating fast and the sound of her breathing deeply, Norma assuaged her, "Sish, Connie – Sish."

Norma then looked knowingly at Culpa with a smile of relief, then looked back at Connie, "Sleep now." She took off her glowing necklace and placed it around Connie's neck to comfort her, and laid her on the wavy, ocean floor where Norma and Culpa waited for Connie when she disappeared into evil hands.

Connie's body felt as though it were to break or crush. Weakly, she turned her head to the right side, and with her right hand, she felt the deep, wavy sands and communicated with Norma, for she hadn't the strength to speak.

"Oh, Norma, I had been so confused when I was with my father, but when I am with you, it is worse --- I do not think that I have been more confused in my life. Please, please ---," as she still touched the wavy sand, "Do not confuse me more than I already am, for I do not know what came over me – to change my mind so that Marrina can be saved. Marrina, Oh, Norma, please, let's go to Marrina soon!" She fell into a deep, restful sleep to heal.

"*Oh, Connie,*" Norma thought. "*I am so grateful and so amazed despite the fact that you're giving up so much and that you're still confused, yet you're still willing to forgive and help Marrina. You put me to shame.*"

Norma chanted a lullaby from Marrina to Connie as she slept

in her arms. Somehow, it echoed to the end of the tunnel. Connie dreams of being a mermaid, and the thought of meeting the mermaids and mermen of Marrina – a place, a magical world made of a kingdom – fulfilled her even unto her dreams.

After Connie awoke, all three, Connie, Norma, and Culpa, began their journey to Marrina. As Connie reached the end of a meadow of seaweed, she sighted a glowing presence that pierced her eyes. As she looked at herself, she found that she was also illuminating as well! With full wonder, she turned and looked to the sides of the dome-shaped tunnel and found that the glittery stones were reflecting her light and made her shine, and made the atmosphere eerily bright. Then, looking at the stranger, who glowed brighter than she, she remained stunned and still. She noted the outline of a woman of shimmering nature materializing front and center of her with a marvelous shimmer!

"Hello, Connie. I am so grateful that you have come," the heavenly figure said. She looked like the brightest angel that came from heaven. Connie was speechless. Her voice sounded so sweet, beautiful, and innocent.

"Please come closer. You seem so far away." Not only did Connie remember those same lines, but she felt déjà vu moment at the same time.

With her eyes as wide as can be, Connie became nervous as they swam deeper into the sea, where the waves of the sand began to become invisible, making Connie more aware that Marrina was very close. Upon looking back, the sea made an extraordinary change – it was much dimmer, but with her mermaid eyes, she could almost see anything and glowed brightly like Culpa, which was frightening the creatures of the dark.

Connie began to notice Culpa's shape. True, she had a tail like theirs, but Culpa seemed to be magical, and she stood out. *"Sailors have seen mermaids out at sea,"* Connie thought, *"but why did they not mention a fairy mermaid? It turns out that they are mermaid companions or helpers. This world seems so strange and mysterious, but why the other moment, I felt like I knew the sea when I was on the earth, and here, it is not like what I imagined or knew at all. It is different and more wonderful at the same time."* She tried to recall where or when she had heard those exact lines.

"Please", the sweetness in her voice was remarkable, bringing the sounds of the waves to her memory. Connie then remembered.....it was the day when she met Norma on the beach. Norma used those exact same words! Only it wasn't Norma this time. Connie was almost sure of it, for if it was Norma, she would have remembered right away.

Connie slowly swam to Norma, keeping her head down, for so many unordinary things had been happening since she became a mermaid. With Connie's frightful eyes nailed to the surface of the tunnel, her eyebrows suddenly wrinkled with absolute amazement. The sign of the dangerous area that Connie had encountered was gone, and there appeared, to her knowledge and sight, the wavy lines on the sand, the sign of the closeness to Marrina.

The glowing hands of the heavenly figure in her vision lifted Connie's head. The mysterious figure had sparkling stars on her face. Keeping her palms on her eyes, which seemed to be a woman's, Connie finally looked up, under the trust of her destiny, blinded, for the figure glowed very brightly.

"Behold!" the mermaid said, "You are only a moment away from the kingdom of my beloved father and of his father before him. This is the kingdom that has been betrayed by the 'Evil One, but most of all, the kingdom that has awaited you."

At that moment, Connie realized that it was Princess Gwendela before her, face to face. Filled with such awe, and closely feeling each one's presence, Connie and Princess Gwendela's eyes were glued on each other in amazement.

Connie's heart fluttered about to and fro till, finally, it stuck in her throat. Weakness crept up on her, making her shiver. The capillaries of her eyes grew large and hard as if she were about to turn into stone.

As her mermaid's eyes overcame the power of such a candle power, her eyes concentrated on Gwendela. Her eyes became fatigued, making Gwendela appear to be different. Colors danced, causing her eyes to become wet and cloudy. Heavy fluids flowed down her cheeks that did not seem to dissolve. Weakly, Connie shook as she tried to touch Princess Gwendela's face with her hands but stopped as she felt life and reason within her mind had slipped away.

Quickly, Princess Gwendela held her steady, taking Connie by the hand to feel her heart's pace. As her hand reached the bottom of her cheek, Connie felt soft pebbles bouncing lightly into her hands. Astonishingly, Connie's eyes were once again wide open. Looking into her hand, she realized that she had cried pearls; something that no human on earth could do.

Gwendela folded her fingers in so that Connie could hold them lightly, close to her heart, for Connie had just seen herself as if she looked into the mirror six years later when she looked into Gwendela's eyes and face. Miraculously, every feature, every shape that was Connie's, was also Gwendela's, except for her purple eyes.

Shadows of the creatures that were summoned to get a hold of Connie slowly approached the throne of the "Evil One." Her flaming pupils anxiously burned with rage. The intensity of such frustration and anger caused the bones of her face to shiver. Nerves within her skin danced vigorously, making the fingers of her hands move like waves. The sound of her heartbeat pounded and echoed throughout her kingdom, amplified by the powers of hell.

Black Eyes of Edom, knowing well of her sister's and Connie's alliance, laughed madly like a wild beast. Her deep voice was overfilled in her lungs with such intense anger, causing them to bleed. She knew that there was only one more way to destroy Connie – only one — and this time, she herself would take care of it.

With entire confidence, the same sly grin appeared on her bloody lips as the beauty of her gorgeous face literally shined, with her fingers playfully twisting her long, black curly hair and childishly biting her bloody lips more.

As their hands engaged, Princess Gwendela and the long-awaited savior of Marrina entered into a world of beauty and mystery, giving Connie absolute fulfillment. She quivered as she emotionally took in every scenic inch that was in front of her, then passed it, and so on, building up emotions of overwhelming fulfillment. Going into the land that she was to save gave her feelings few humans have experienced: feelings of love, relief, anxiousness, great honor, and fright of what was expected of her, all at once. This feeling made her feel as if she would literally explode, making the grasp of their hands tighter.

As they kept on swimming deeper into the tunnel approaching the entrance of Marrina, the atmosphere was changing. They were swimming deep down at a steep angle, giving Connie a feeling as if there was no ground beneath her. Upon looking at their held hands, Connie strangely felt a radiance of great power, love, and beauty and felt reassured again.

Connie's spine trembled from having emotions of such depth, the feeling of finally being in Marrina, but the back of her mind was the feeling of fright.

The feelings and thoughts that raced in her mind suddenly stopped. She realized what was in front of her – the beautiful sight of Marrina.

Right there and then, Connie heavenly closed her eyes just once, only once to reach down within her to gather courage, and promised herself and God that she would not falter. With a smile on her face, Connie grabbed hold of her heart for this awesome moment and felt happy, completely happy. Gently grabbing her hand once again, Princess Gwendela, the princess of this hidden world, led Connie into the vast land of her beloved father.

Marrina glowed uniquely, like the sun, the moon, and the stars all into one; the dashing glow looked unworldly. Up at a good distance, Connie could see a gigantic pearl of cream color. With her wide eyes open, Connie looked at the beautiful, gigantic pearl. She gasped when she felt a tug at her fins, which caused her to look down. She feasted her eyes on an adorable, young, innocent face, making her want to weep. The young one's aqua blue eyes were big and deep as deep as well and as big as a church door, and her smiling young red lips made her cheeks look like round lollipops.

Her smile went away as she looked at Gwendela. Connie felt uncomfortable, feeling as though she scared the poor little mermaid. Connie looked into the young girl's eyes; then the girl said.

"Mommy?" the little girl's voice quivered. Her adorable face looked saddened with her forehead wrinkled in pain. Connie could feel Gwendela talking to the little girl's mind. The girl started crying tears of white liquid. Surprised, Connie looked down at the ground of Marrina and watched pearls land. Looking up, Connie remembered and thought of Princess Gwendela when she lost her mother, but most of all, when Connie lost her own mother.

Filled with compassion, Connie quickly picked up the crying little mermaid and hugged her as tight as she could. With her eyes closed, Connie knew the feeling and was surprised by the little mermaid when she hugged her back with even more intensity.

Her voice unexpectedly crept into Connie's mind, not her ear, saying with her sweet voice echoing, "Welcome, Connie. I love you, our hope.

At that moment, Connie knew the depth of her mission. Then Connie laid the little mermaid down.

"All the time I am with you, I feel like bursting and shouting out to God that I have a mermaid as a sister!" Connie exclaimed with such joy to Princess Gwendela.

CHAPTER 9

Connie's eyes were opened to the new world. Both Princess Gwendela and Connie journeyed around Marrina together, and the glowing light looked like a projection of an alternative heaven that embellished Marrina's waters. A sense of pure platinum life surrounded every inch, but so did a sense of worry and terror of when the Black Eyes of Edom and her creatures would strike again.

Connie paraded on a golden coach wagon pulled by large sea horses decked with all manner of ornamentation. The people of Marrina offered their little dwellings made of glittering sand and slivery streets mostly of what they expected of the hope-to-be savior Connie, and every hand humbly offered love to her.

Their little dwellings were made of glittery sand from the very ground of wavy lines, which was a symbol close to Connie in every moment, but in the back of her mind, that growing fear of the princess of evil and the fear of her own life being taken away by almost overtook Connie.

The glittery sand that made up the dwellings, shells and stones mixed together and formed the hard coverage; little pea plants that were spread out on the ocean floor moved like long grains of wheat, and as tiny segments of flying organisms flew above. Connie waited for a moment with a sense of peacefulness and beauty, looking at this beautiful but strange sight of paradise.

With great longing, Connie just had to fall on her mermaid tail and grab with her fingers the sand of Marrina. With the other hand, she put across her heart to see if she was really alive. Then, out of nowhere, she heard giggling and looked up with her mermaid eyes. At that instant, she felt and could see the difference -- her eyes had sharpened since she had been in the sea.

"Of course you are alive!" Princess Gwendela laughed good-heartedly.

Connie just stood there looking at her very oddly, almost ready to burst with joyful laughter. Gwendela's laugh sounded so much like the sea of life, but her sister's laugh sounded like the sea of death; such a huge difference that one would not have the slightest guess that they were both sisters!

Princess Gwendela's smile turned the opposite at the thought of Connie. Connie sees Gwendela in pain. The Princess's face trembled. She tried to stop, but she couldn't help it. Her eyes looked tired from all the times she was sad and so frightened of her own sister, who was once Princess Matropula.

Connie felt guilt draping her whole body, but suddenly a voice came from within telling her that guilt would get her nowhere, only strength and confidence. With strength and confidence, she will save Marrina.

Connie, all of a sudden, heard a big slam near her and spontaneously looked down at the ground, but didn't know why. The light in Marrina started to look like a strange heaven and began to dim.

"Connie!" Princess Gwendela exclaimed as she lay on the ground. "Please, please help us!"

There was so much weight upon the princess, and she looked so helpless like someone or something was pulling her down. That gave Connie the desperation to want to help her. Connie's eyes were wide open as she tried to look at the princess's eyes after she knelt beside her, not knowing what to do.

"Gwendela, Princess Gwendela!" Connie said anxiously, shaking her peach-colored shoulders, still looking deep into her eyes.

Gwendela's breath was heavy and filled with such constriction that she kept on coughing and felt pain in her gills as her eyes widened.

"Connie, you feel the truth. You know the truth, but you cannot see it," Gwendela gasped.

"Gwendela?" Connie longed.

"It is too late for me, oh Connie. You are so special. Fight, Just fight." Gwendela coughed.

"NO!"

"Yes."

Connie was trembling with such fear, feeling weakness sneak into her soul.

"But Princess Gwendela, you are special, too!" Connie pleaded.

"Poor Connie, you don't even know your own strength..." Princess Gwendela couldn't say another word. The pain inside her was too strong.

Guilt again draped Connie's mermaid body.

"No!" Connie told herself in anguish. As she still looked at Gwendela, who looked lifeless. She dramatically threw her arms around her with such love and hurt that the muscles of her throat went dry.

As her mind began to create a storm of fear, she just had to grab a hold of her head with both of her hands tightly, with almost complete then she looked up and saw the glowing pearl – the Pearl of Marrina – its shape was so perfect, so safe, with such an appeal that surrounded it. She looked down at Princess Gwendela. She wavered over which way to turn and heard the laughter of someone with a deep voice.

"Stop doing this to Marrina!" Connie ordered, but the laughter grew louder and louder. Connie knew that laughter. The mermaids and mermen were swimming in every direction in such chaos. They all had their own strengths, but they were just running away.

"I need to do something," Connie told herself. "I will not let this…" She could not think straight.

Then she, herself, began to feel the weight on top of her, trying to drag her down. Connie kept swaying her head. She didn't know where else to turn, so she fell to the ground out of desperation.

"God, please help me!" Connie prayed weakly; her whole body was almost glued to the glittery, wavy sand. "Oh, God!"

Her right hand glowed brightly through her, but she didn't notice at first. She just had her lips on the sand, and then, with her left desperate hand, she clenched the sea floor. The glow then slowly blinded her eyes and traveled up into her head. Connie could not believe it!

"Could this be true?" Connie thought weakly.

"Stand up. Stand up!" An almighty voice demanded.

"NO," Connie whimpered cowardly; Connie wanted to crawl under a rock. Who was this voice that commanded her so, Connie thought frightfully.

"In your heart, you know," the almighty voice said, "Now arise and receive "Providence." The voice was not all of demand but also reassuring and determined.

At that, Connie arose from the ground, but she felt totally unworthy of having encountered Deity. The Being of Source is above all creatures, evil or good. Yes, in her heart, she knew who this voice was and quickly obeyed her Higher Power. God.

The glow of Deity traveled to a part of her chest until it flowed over the interior of her body, with the sense of power over-whelming her so much that it caused her to blink her eyes in total amazement. She felt so complete, and truly, she was complete. The confidence and strength that she thought she never had over-powered her whole body, making her look like a beautiful jewel, and the facets were the innocence of her soul.

At the epiphany of her transfiguration, she dazzled. Every cry that shrieked slowly died down. Connie looked down humbly, for she knew the change well and knew how beautiful she looked and how beautiful she felt. The sense of purity and piety overtook her so that she could taste it with her lips. All the mermaids and mermen stopped, and silence filled the land. The rumbling of the evil entity that tried to take over the land of Marrina desisted in dire defeat.

Slowly, Connie looked up in such great awe, that only the angels of heaven could describe it. Deeply she swallowed and saw every weary eye of Marrina look upon her, and all gratefully acknowledged her as they swam towards their hope-to-be savior.

Gently, she smiled upon them, but the wrinkled corners of her mouth were filled with pity. Nevertheless, she held her head up straight and said, "Marrina!" The confidence and strength that overwhelmed her was apparent from the sternness of her voice.

"I was called to serve you, Marrians, and that I shall. But I cannot do this alone, for this is your land, Marrina! You must help your queen, Princess Gwendela, for her sister, the "Evil One," has weakened her." All looked down and finally noticed their princess, and the mermaids began to whine.

"You must stop this," Connie insisted as gently as she could, "Princess Gwendela needs your strength and courage – not your pearls."

How mighty Connie looked, and she looked just like Princess Gwendela, especially at this moment.

"Oh, dear savior Connie," they all cried, "What can we do?"

Trying to contain herself from such overwhelming sympathy, Connie bit her lips, and at that moment, the motherless little mermaid who cried for her mother came and comfortably rested in Connie's arms. Holding her warmly, an inspiration overcame her as the little mermaid whispered childishly, in Connie's mind, beautiful songs that were unknown to man. Finally, the little mermaid revealed her name which turned out to be "Resona."

Her voice was sweet and mellow as Connie answered, "Go

first and take your sleeping princess in her glowing palace, The Great Pearl and take her into her chambers to rest."

"I shall do this," answered a young merman. Connie smiled and willingly nodded with approval.

The nice and devoted young mermaid gave a grateful smile and lifted her princess to the palace as Connie had requested.

Still, all eyes were on Connie's gaze, and once more, Connie earnestly aided by saying, "You shall have refuge and strength, and it will come from each other, and you shall not foster chaos amongst yourselves."

"But my dear Connie," pleaded a weeping merman, "What can we do that we have not already tried?" This merman seemed bitter beneath his pleas and very sad. His hair was braided slickly in the back, and shells held the braid together. He looked weak and defeated.

Inspiration arrived to her from an unknown source, and she answered, "Good and innocent souls of Marrina, you don't even know your own strength!"

Pearls were spilling from every eye that looked upon her gaze, but the little mermaid in Connie's arms was strong with the faith that there was hope in the loving arms that held her gently, for it had been a long time since she felt safe in anyone's arms.

Despite the weaknesses of Marrina, Connie did not let go of her own strength, which empowered her. Just then, the power of the strength of her inspiration gently left her to feed their weaknesses, forming glittery rays around themselves.

This magical moment held every tear back from their eyes. As the young merman came from the palace from placing Princess Gwendela in the Great Pearl, he looked surprisingly at Connie and then at his family. A joyful smile was placed on his mother's deep red lips. Then he hugged his closest relative – his mother.

"Oh, Mother!" he cried out with such desperation and want.

Everyone slowly started to feel such happiness. Joy filled their hearts and souls, and everything that was sad and awful changed into dance and song as Connie humbly looked at them in child-like ways.

They all formed a circle, holding hands around Connie and the child,

"Oh, thanks be to God.
To our Savior, most High
For He brought Connie, the dear one, to us
He who instructed and entrusted her
To fill our hearts, Marrians, with strength
And the joy of the Lord!

They all sang this song with their sea instruments. A merman, who was humble of feature and movements, came with his instrument, with his old, piercing gray eyes. He smiled up at Connie as he recognized her for her greatness and strength. The elderly merman nodded his head gently and introduced himself.

"I am Rumty," the pleasant merman said. As he said his name, he stressed the 'R' in a rattling tone with the vibration of his tongue.

With great passion in his eyes, he softly places a long, tubular coral on the end of his lips. Such sweet melodic tones and undertones unravel out of the small openings as he drew each breath from his gills. Bubbles from the openings of his fine flute filled their ears, and all were in delighted bliss.

Then, a strange feeling came over Connie. As this beautiful music dwelt deeper and deeper into her soul, the tiniest speck of her hidden doom was replaced with the longing that this magnificent music offered. It gave her such a strong desire to help them that the pity that she had for them was turning into compassion, and the grip that she had on the child that she held grew stronger.

Her love grew stronger, and the music was filled with longing yet full of hope.

Suddenly, there was dead silence; everyone was still, and not even the slightest motion was made. There was a huge, hollow rumble beneath them. Each hand dug their fingers into the glowing sands of Marrina, out of the longing to live peacefully, for they knew who was trembling their hearts, their homes, their waters, and their land, Marrina.

The shaking created a roar below them, and each creature – snails, crabs, fish, and every living thing under the sea -- was being cast aside as the ground of Marrina opened. There, sprung out of the ground, was the evil princess, Black Eyes of Edom.

CHAPTER 10

This time, Black Eyes of Edom was not dressed in fine jewels, or pearls draping down her neck, as Connie had remembered rather only with her large garments and one gown that she wore with the colors of black, red, and dark blue. Since darkness filled the land, her fiery red pupils were burning with a sinister desire to extricate Connie, which was the last destruction she had sinfully hoped and waited upon.

She looked more terrifying. Her sharp front teeth were now fangs covering her bloody red lower lip. Her wickedness consumed her which caused great alarm and pain to those who are weak of soul. So intense was this ugly evil within her that it poisoned her moral and environmental existence.

"Look!" one mermaid cried, "Horns are growing out of her very head!" At this overwhelming sight, many mermaids fainted to a collapsed drop.

"Bonthenal," he whispered lovingly to his mate. "I shall not let this beast harm you."

Just then, Connie felt terror within her, not so much as a weak coward would feel, but at the awareness of a huge, powerful devil such as she is. This awareness of Connie created a righteous anger within her. Slowly, Connie put down the little mermaid and carefully placed her in an elderly mermaid's arms. The little mermaid tried to resist by being feisty.

"Connie!" she shouted with worry. "Do not go away. I am frightened!" The little mermaid's eyes were in a daze of terror for their lives.

"She must go. She is our hope-to-be- savior," the elderly mermaid said slowly, but her heart ached at the state of the little mermaid, and she remembered what had happened to the little one's mother; she was captured by Black Eyes of Edom's soldiers, they took her away, and they never saw her again. It was known in their land, Marrina, that once captured, you were tortured, and then your life was taken away savagely.

Connie slowly approached Black Eyes of Edom without a flinch of fear in her eyes. Her throat tensed up in awe, for Black Eyes of Edom was four times the size of Connie. The evil witch held a long spear that was in the shape of a three pronged wicked branch tree. In its openings were the dwellings of sea micro-organisms. At the top of this mighty, long and unusual spear was the head of a sea monster. Its head was in the shape of an alligator, and sharp, pointy fangs were there jotting out of the mouth. It was in an attack position as if it was ready to bite or tear. Nevertheless, Connie kept a strong stance, with her spirit ever strengthening with purity and sternness.

The power between them was incredible. The sight of them was an awesome moment; the people of Marrina stared at these two mighty, opposing powers. Every eye that looked upon them was filled with hope, justice, and, most of all, anticipation for the long awaited event was actually happening!

"What is it that you want from this precious land of Marrina?" asked Connie firmly.

"You foolish, silly, ignorant little mortal!" the princess snapped angrily, "You had a chance to leave this miserable place and go to your father in your own land, but NO, you had to meddle"!

"I meddled with my heart out of love for these your people,"

Connie interrupted, humbly bending her head lowly. Connie grew aware of the evil one did not understand her heart. The evil one did not understand that her heart only had a will to love and to sacrifice. Connie could feel it within the depths of her soul that the evil one had not such a heart as hers, and with that,, she lifted her head mightily and with righteousness, and for once, she felt she had one advantage this time.

"Well, if it wasn't for your heart," the princess exaggerated, bending down to meet Connie's eyes, "then there would have been no need for me to have...well, how would one say this...make plans for the burial of your poor servant, Norma!"

At that, Connie was actually stunned — bewildered at the realization that she had almost forgotten about Norma.

"*Norma!*" Connie quickly thought, "*Oh, my poor Norma. She guided me and loved me. Why, she was like a mother to me!*"

"How dare you!" Connie manageably exclaimed.

Her human nature took its course, for she was gravely hurt and impulsively acted upon it.

"You are lying!" she added quickly, "You are nothing but a predator filled with nothing but deceit and the ugliest of evil." Connie didn't catch her righteous words but felt the blow that hit across the evil one's face.

The people of Marrina triumphantly roared with the sound of cheer, making Connie blink blindly. She had never slapped anyone in her life with such harsh words. She then looked automatically back towards Black Eyes of Edom but only saw the slight twitch of the end of the left corner of her mouth.

"You have done enough to these poor, innocent people. And as of now, your plan of total destruction over Marrina is over. Done with." Connie said with such passionate exasperation. "You will never, in the name of God, will never harm Marrina or its people. Again!!"

———

With her evil wand of snakes and eels, Black Eyes of Edom aimed the dire wand and an unusual laser that consisted of fire and, at the same time, somehow was traveling toward Connie. Connie was in her 'God Zone.' She saw the incoming laser and focused, "I and my God are one, and now God alone is here, and I am not!" Transfixed Connie with God's power, the laser flames leave Connie unscathed- free from burns and sears. Black Eyes of Edom is stunned and unnerved, seeing that Connie is unaffected. She wonders and aiming her laser at the life around Marrina, she blasts, and sure enough, everything else in Marrina is ablaze, but why not Connie and the innocent lives? Ignoring her better judgment, she again aims at Connie, but the fire quickly goes back to Black Eyes of Edom, and she receives a nasty wound. Marrina's people and Culpa are astonished to see Black Eyes of Edom folded over in pain. Then, they all realize that Connie is indeed more powerful.

Connie was now conscious of her power and was now in a hyper zone of Deity. Black Eyes of Edom, with difficulty, reaches for a different wand and again aims it at Connie as she gets to her feet. But this wand is armed with snakes and eels ,all of which are anxious to inflict their deadly bites. As they approach, Connie grabs the wand by its' lower end and throws it back at Black Eyes of Edom. Black Eyes sees their approach, is helpless, and realizes disaster. The wand of creatures rips chunks of her flesh, and the Black Eyes of Edom is soon reduced to a gooey batter. Connie is encased in light, and then the Marrians see that she normalizes. She talks to them somberly but with a slight smile. "It is finished, and your pain and suffering will now turn to joy. Weep no more! The witch is dead. Now you can live and rest and play and be yourselves and remember that God did this for you and not I. He just used me as if I were a hammer-that's all!

An evil cry of defeat finally came out of the mouth of Black Eyes of Edom. She was swallowed whole, disappearing from the now beautiful light of Marrina. Everyone of Marrina shouted for joy and relief for Black Eyes of Edom was no more. All of their cruel suffering had come to an end.

The colors of the blackish blue box exploded in Connie's mind. This memory will never go away. The memory of this magnificent sea and the beautiful sea stories behind it, for Connie had made history in the sea. Facing Black Eyes of Edom, who was the most powerful of evil creatures known to the sea, was destroyed. Feelings of deep longing to go back to the earth overcame her. She hid deep within her. But now alive was the overwhelming feeling of saving the land of Marrina. She procured the freedom of the Marrians, and it was her destiny.

"Now our world will be safe from the strong clutches of evil, free from a horrible hook," Norma thought to herself. Norma further thought to herself, *"Now, Connie. You can go home. I don't think that she will wish to stay with us and further guide or rule this land"*.

Connie approached Norma, "Dearest.

Norma, I must go I must go back to my home, to my father. I don't know what's become of him. I must seek him out and tend to him."

"We all know you must go home," replied Princess Gwendela. "for I have to awaken from a deep slumber to find Marrina safe and sound. Soon, you will finally be safe and sound in your world. Connie, I am proud of you. And one more thing. You will never be forgotten."

CHAPTER 11

For once, Connie understood everything. Everything that seemed to be a fantasy was beginning to be so real, too real. At this very moment, the sea was no longer a stranger to her.

Connie proudly looked at the fish that passed by her, but her heart was heavier than before. As Norma took Connie by the hand, Culpa followed behind as they journeyed deeper into the sea to the nexus of the beautiful land, Marrina.

There they arrived at a destination, Connie wondered to herself, "What part of Marrina is this?"

"It is the center of where we believe that our creation started. You must drink of this waterfall and bath in it as well, then you will become human, yet with our help....and in doing so, you will be able to withstand the air of humans, returning to your land.....in your own human body."

"But I cannot return!" Connie exclaimed, "I must save Marrina!"

"But you already have," Norma said earnestly. Connie kept shaking her head in fearful disbelief. "Remember. Remember when I told you that you must prove to our land and our people that you must show that fear can be conquered?! You thought that we may have had to go to war with Princess Matropula. By becoming a mermaid, taking a chance to be in new surroundings, and risking your life, you have saved ours. Don't you know that Black Eyes of Edom is no longer Black Eyes of Edom? It is only by peace that fear and destruction can be desist. Only peace and love can change hearts, and that is true courage. Your mission is complete. And we all know now you must go now. Please...the Gate of Time will leave for another year here, which is ten in your land. Please, Connie. Trust me. Your servant."

"I want to stay. I, too, am a Marrian," Connie sobbed, wanting not to let go of Norma's hand, yet knew she had to go home to her father and brother.

"You will," Norma said as simply as she could. "Marrina will always be in your heart. It always has been."

Connie turned towards the water to enter the timeless waterfall. Then, she looked back for Norma, who was gone from her sight. Just as she was alone in her decision to save Marrina, so was she again alone in returning to the family who first loved and knew her.

Voices kept repeating her name in a calling desperate manner. With flashes of light streaming down her body, during the transformation to her humanity, she felt no pain. Just peace and love all around......

"Over here! I spotted her, Mr. Thomas!" a police officer cried out on the sandy beach.

Connie had on the same clothes in which she left her house. Yet her whole body was wet, wrapped in long green seaweed.

"Oh, thank God!!!!!!! Connie!" Mr. Thomas exclaimed, "My angel of a daughter. My God, MY God...Thank you, Jesus, for bringing her safe back to me..."Connie is still looking unconscious. "Connie. Connie. Connie. Look at daddy!"

Connie slowly opened her eyes with a peaceful smile as if she were a sleeping beauty who had rested in a land of dreams and miracles.

"Daddy?"

That marked an ending of an era. Connie grew more from the experience of saving Marrina. She realized there is an answer for everything, even if it's no or not at this time. She kept her experience to herself, fearing no one would believe her.

From the eighth grade,, she climbed the success ladder and wanted to climb higher beyond her 12th year of high school. Connie graduated as valedictorian of her class. His father was proud. Her brother Joey joined the Marines, which shocked Connie and her father Mr. Thomas.

Connie's journey in life seemed to be of lessons of the heart. The heart can be a tricky thing and yet her faith grew. Facing the world without a mother only made her stronger.

And now, it's the graduation commencement ceremony at Ray high school, and Connie is the Valedictorian. She is getting ready for her speech to her classmates when a tear of self-love trickles. It seems that after her Marrian dark adventure, tears come to Connie so much easier.

Tears ran down her cheek, remembering at once upon a time when she was underneath the seagulls' flight in the salty waters leading to Marrina, and she cried pearls. Marrina was in her blood, and never would she betray the memory of Marrina.

The valedictorian stepped up the stairs of the auditorium, which was surrounded by applause and approached the podium at her high school graduation. She had a tablet in her hands, also carrying her heart of gold. Wearing a blue cap and gown, she also wore medals of achievement around her neck. Her lips parted, and she began her speech:

Each and everyone this year has a story to tell. And I have mine. The biggest dilemma I have faced growing up in the classroom is fear. Yes, even I had inner problems that I had to face. I, too, had my insecurities about becoming an adult, yet fear kept me down. With the challenges each day would bring, I looked more at the positives in my life, which helped me succeed academically. Yet there were also days that I was just downright terrible. Sound familiar? I sound like you? Don't I? The point I am trying to make is that in our humanness we all have our strengths and weaknesses. We are all a group trying to reach one common goal. Happiness. We have a common thread that links us together.

Whatever route we take, whatever road we travel on, it is very clear that we are one and the same. We breathe the same air. So, instead of fighting with each other, we need to realize and respect each other's dignity, knowing we all come from the same source. God. Keeping this in mind, I will boldly say that I am not the only Valedictorian here today. We are all Valedictorians in our own right. We were all striving for the same thing to graduate. I took the same classes as you did. Just think of me as the message-buler. And I am glad to be one. With that, I will close, and God Bless you all.

There was a roar of applause. She received a standing ovation. Everyone was moved, especially her father.

Connie went to college in town to study Marine Biology. College for her was an experience she could never forget. She made close friends quickly in her field of study. Everyone was studying Marine Biology for different reasons; however, Connie's reason was to protect the sea environment and to start her own organization to protect sea life to promote more respect and appreciation for the wonders of the ocean. Although Connie's new mission was rare and not a big money business, Connie felt so strongly about what she was doing that she formed a small club on campus, which grew large in a year's time.

Once she graduated from college with a Bachelor's Degree in Marine Biology, she decided to stay on the home front. She took a job position with the museum in town as a Marine Specialist, and within two years, she had her dream- her own non-profit organization. She named it *Marrina's Life Support.* She later learned that this was a Spanish name for marine life.

Connie was not only influential in the community but also proud.

Beneath the waters that lead to Marinna, there was peace and tranquility. Princess Gewndela and her older sister, Princess Matropula, reigned over the growing land in population. By now Marrina and had grown twice its size; all were united. The waters promoted peace and tranquility over, shadowing their dark past that was so much in turmoil. The difference is so vast that the evil past was very much forgotten. Yet Connie wasn't forgotten. Connie was held in their loving memory. So much was their appreciation that there was a monument, a statue in resemblance to Connie, built in her honor. It was a tall statue in the middle of Marinna on the very spot where Black Eyes of Eden challenged Connie. Everyone that swam by smiled in great confidence that nothing like this could ever happen again inside or outside the realms of Marrina because they had Connie speaking up for them, defending their waters for miles and miles ahead. Oh yes, the people of Marrina kept up with what the earthling did.

Princess Gwendela came before the statue of Connie and recalled everything that had happened. Norma came right beside Princess Gwendela, and they both began to speak of their gratitude and great love for Connie. The waters of Marrina reached Connie's heart, and she felt their love. And yet all that dear Connie went through: in her earthly life, and her small visit from earth to the sandy waters of Marrina, she could never forget her purpose then and now. And that is to sacrifice her very self in helping to save an unknown world from destruction and pain. *Marrina.*

The End